I0527258

Code Mercy

Amanda Huot

ISBN: 979-8-218-41245-6

Dedication:

This book is dedicated to all hospital chaplains around the world, including the ladies at St. Joseph's hospital in Nashua, as well as Bill Sweeney and Sr. Martha over at Catholic Medical Center, who bring peace, comfort, and empathy to patients and families in their darkest hours. Your work does not go unnoticed. Thank you for all you do.

Chapter 1

"Oh, for goodness' sake." Jacki muttered to herself. She had already spilled her coffee, dropped a pile of papers on the floor, and now seemed to be hitting every red light on the way to work. It's Monday! Jacki hoped that this would not be an inclination as to how the rest of her Monday would be. Once she arrived at the hospital, found a parking spot, and got into the building, she could tell it would be a crazy day. The ED bays were completely full, and the last shift she worked, the hospital was already at 95% capacity. Taking a breath, she hopped into an elevator and headed to the morning meeting with the Spiritual Care staff.

Jacki listened as Kathryn, the head of Spiritual Care, briefed the staff on all the day's cases, waiting for her name to be called. The morning meeting, unlike other staff members, was Jacki's favorite time of the day, as it allowed her time to talk with other chaplains and gave her a clear direction for her day's agenda.

"Jacki- I hate to do this to you, but I'm giving you a lot of cases today. There are two patients in ICU that need pastoral counseling, one is at end-of-life stages but is alert and able to communicate. I also have you assigned to visit the SUD wing, you have one patient in the McKinley center who is requesting a female chaplain, and I also have you assigned to be the on call for the ED." Jacki jokingly rolled her eyes and sighed at Kathryn as she took the large case load from her. Kathryn truly felt horrible for giving her so many cases but knew she could handle it. "Thanks, Kathryn. Please don't worry about giving me lots of cases, you know I enjoy my work."

The staff closed their meeting with a prayer and disbursed to their respective units. Jacki immediately went to the hospital coffee shop to replace the coffee that she had spilled on herself. As much as I love my job, just looking at this heavy stack of cases calls for a tall, strong iced coffee! She then went to her office to skim all her cases.

ICU W2: Ronald Caruso, 50. End stage Kidney cancer. No longer taking treatment. Requesting spiritual care to ask questions regarding what comes next. Raised Catholic but fell away during his college years. Married with two adult children.

ICU N4: Patryk Kennedy. Age 45. Victim of severe car accident. Paralyzed and non-verbal as result of accident. Family requesting consult with Spiritual Care regarding removing him from life support. Devout

Catholic family questioning if ending life support is against their beliefs. Have consulted priests and given conflicting answers.

McKinley Room 4: Emma Bryne 15. End stage Ovarian Cancer. Angry at God but wants to talk to a female chaplain. Father accepts that his daughter is dying, mother is devoutly religious and refuses to accept that her

daughter is entering hospice. Emma does believe in God but is struggling with accepting her diagnosis at a young age.

Jacki put down Emma's folder and sighed. She felt for Emma, as she had a high school friend who also was diagnosed with Ovarian Cancer at a young age, and ultimately passed away from it. God, please give me the words to comfort her, let me be patient with her, and not insult or judge her for being upset with you. Bless my time with all these patients today, as well as the ones I have yet to know about. Give me the strength and the grace to reach their hearts for your glory, even in the smallest ways. Amen.

Jacki decided to save Emma for last and headed over to Ronald in ICU West. She would visit the SUD wing after Patryk, and then end with Emma. Of course, this could easily change at the drop of a dime, being that she was also ED chaplain on call. But this was always her plan of action, to at least plan out her assignments based on need. She threw her empty coffee cup in the wastebasket and went off towards the stairs to head to ICU.

Rounding the corner from the stairs, Jacki headed to the West wing of the ICU, where patients who were somewhat stable, or able to communicate, were kept. She knocked softly on Ronald's door. "Come in!" A male and female voice echoed in tandem. Jacki swung the door open gently, closing it behind her. "Hello, Ronald. I'm Jacki, one of the chaplains here." Looking over at what she presumed was Ronald's wife, she smiled, "I'm sorry, I was not given your name. Are you Ronald's wife.?" Smiling, the woman nodded. "Yes! My name is Janette. Nice to meet you." Jacki smiled and returned her attention to Ronald.

"Ronald, my notes here say you are in the end stages of kidney cancer, have refused further treatment, and have questions regarding what comes next?" Ronald cleared his throat and

looked away from his wife. "Yeah, I was raised Catholic and taught about when you die, you go home to the Lord and see all your loved ones, but I fell away in my younger years. We raised our kids Catholic, but I never was the devout father. Janette took the kids through all their courses and sacraments, I just attended at Christmas and Easter and at big events…." His voice trailed off and Jacki thought she saw a tear streaming down his face. She walked closer to him and gently sat on the chair next to his bed.

"So…now you're questioning if God is going to treat you with the same coldness you realize you gave him?"

Janette seemed slightly taken aback by Jacki's abruptness, but Ronald smiled and let out a small chuckle. "Yeah, exactly."

"Well, Ronald. I am not God, so I suppose I can't directly tell you what to believe. I was raised Catholic, too, but fell away for my own reasons. What I've learned in my new faith walk, is that the only true requirement for our salvation is that we believe and accept Jesus into our hearts. Do you believe in him, Ronald? Do you believe he died for you, and forgave you of your sins?"

Ronald seemed a little squeamish at those questions, and Jacki took note of it. She wondered if the hesitation was due to Janette being there. Just when she was about to ask Janette to step out for a moment, Ronald suddenly responded. "I do. I always did. My belief was there, but I just couldn't catch on to the action part of it. I was your typical man, work and football were more important than going to church. Janette didn't really care what mass or even what church we went to, but I still chose not to attend any. Sometimes…I wonder if that's why I am where I am today." Jacki caught a glimpse of Janette's reaction to that last admission. She inhaled and turned away, but not before Jacki saw her eyes glisten with tears. Ronald noticed, too. Looking at his wife, Ronald added, "she hates when I say that. And I know God doesn't work that way. But guilt messes with your head sometimes, especially when you must stare at these walls all day. Knowing the end is coming, but never knowing when." Jacki nodded in agreement. "Yes, Satan plays with our minds when it comes to making us feel at fault for horrible things like cancer. I'm truly sorry you and your family are going through this. I can't heal you, but I can help you take the steps to heal your soul, so you can leave this world as peacefully as possible and enter the next without any of those chains of guilt. How about I come back tomorrow, and we can discuss more?"

For the first time during their entire visit, Ronald smiled. "I would like that. You know, I was a little hesitant when they told me the chaplain taking my case was a woman. No offense, or anything, but growing up Catholic, I always associated chaplains with priests, and thought if I had a woman chaplain it would be some new age chick coming in with crystals and buddha bellies to rub. But you know your stuff, and I feel you'll really help me." They all shared a laugh, and Jacki smiled. "Thank you, Ronald. I most definitely am not a new ager, and no hard feelings." She turned to Janette with a loving gaze. "Chaplains are not just here for the patient, even in hospital settings. Is there anything I can do for you? How are you doing?" Janette sighed and looked away. Ronald found this concerning. Not wanting to alarm him, she said, "Can I talk to you outside for a minute?" Sensing the tone in her voice, Jacki knew this was something Ronald did not know about. "Of course. We will be right back, Ronald."

When they left the room, Jacki pointed towards the window in the corner, away from earshot. "What is on your mind, Janette?" "Please, call me Nette. It's what everyone else calls me." Jacki nodded and made a note of that but did not respond. Instead, she looked gently at Janette, encouraging her to share. "Well, Ronald doesn't know it, but our daughter Maggie is very upset with him. She's struggling to understand why this is happening, I think, but also holds a lot against her father. You see, it wasn't just church stuff he missed. He seemed to only go to our son's events. Our daughter's choir concerts, or theater productions, didn't mean anything to him. He always had to work on those days, but never our son's. I tried to tell her that sometimes men are like that, but it didn't comfort her very well. Now that he's, well, you're a chaplain I don't have to explain, she's saying she doesn't want to see him, or say goodbye. I can understand how she feels, but it hurts me to see her like this. We raised both our children to respect us, even when it's not easy. I just don't know what to do anymore, I know one day she will regret not seeing him. I've been there with my own parents. Can you help her?"

By the time Janette was done explaining, she could see that she was trying hard to keep her composure. Jacki could feel for her. And Maggie. "How old is Maggie? And how old is your son? How is he handling this?" "Maggie's 20. Our son, Daniel, is 22. He is doing better than Maggie. Dan's already come to say his goodbyes before he left for his semester at college. He calls his father weekly and talks to me regularly too to get updates on his condition." Jacki sighed. "20 is a hard age, Janette. I'm sure it wasn't easy for you at that time. Underneath all the pain and bitterness, I'm sure Maggie is also dealing with her own 'pre-death grieving', thinking about more events he will miss, like her wedding. Does Maggie know that you were going to talk to the chaplain about this? I'm here to help all of you, but I also do not want to make matters worse." Janette looked away for a moment before replying. "I told her I would. She wasn't happy about it, but before I left to come here, she said she would talk if the chaplain was a female." Jacki nodded. "Understandable. I would be happy to meet with her." Jacki reached into her coat pocket to pull out a business card. "My cell phone number is on there. She is free to text or call me anytime. I would love to set up a time to meet with her, and maybe your son as well. But I do have other clients to see, so let's head back into the room." Janette agreed, gave Jacki a small hug, and the two of them made their way back into Ronald's room.

Being the jokester that he was, Ronald looked up and said, "well about time you two come back, I was beginning to think you deserted me!" Jacki smiled, "No, Ronald. We would never desert you. Your wife just had some concerns she wanted to discuss with me away from your room." Ronald nodded. "I see. Well, I hope whatever it was you were able to help her with. I look forward to our visit tomorrow, Jacki. It is refreshing to see young women entering the chaplaincy field." Jacki smiled gracefully, "Thank you, Ronald. That means a lot to me. My family wasn't very supportive of me entering this field. But I knew it was my calling, and I was not going to let anybody deter me from following it. I look forward to our visit tomorrow, too." Jacki closed the door behind her, found a quiet corner in the hallway and sat on the chair to do her notes. After she was done recording her notes on her initial visit, she paused a moment, thinking of Maggie: God, please give me the words to help her. She's so young and going through so much. Anger, bitterness, pre-grieving her future without her father. Guide me as I minister to her, Ronald, and his entire family during this period. Please calm the doubts in my heart that I can help this young woman. You have called me to this field, and I know you will equip me with what is needed. In this case, and all my cases."

Jacki had just closed her surface when she heard her pager go off. She ran to find the nearest phone. "Hey, it's Jacki. You paged me?" "Hi Jacki. It's Anna down in ED. We just had a mass incident come in, school bus coming back from a field trip. Most of the injuries are minor, but there is one student that was hurt badly. His parents are requesting a chaplain." "I'll be right down."

Heading down to the ED, Jacki tried to brace herself for what she might see. There were a variety of options---he could be missing a leg, he could be bleeding out, he could be a small child, a teenager. His parents could simply be anxious and overreacting. As she turned the corner, Jacki could see that her last thought was not the case. Oh, dear. Jacki's adrenaline kicked in and she ran the last few steps towards the trauma bay.

"Hello, I'm Jacki, the chaplain on call for the ED today. I was told you wanted to see a chaplain?" The mother tried to introduce herself but couldn't get a word out without crying. Jacki looked into her eyes before turning her attention to the father. "I'm sure this is not where you are wanting to be. Can you explain to me what's going on?" "I'm sorry, my wife is just so beside herself. You see, Jeffrey is our only child. We tried for many years, but she just kept losing them. Finally, Jeffrey was born healthy, and he's been the pride of our lives. We can't believe this happened. Why us?" Jacki listened intently. "I can't imagine how you must be feeling. I'm sorry for all your losses. I'm a firm believer that pregnancy loss is one of the hardest sorrows to walk through. And now this. I'm sorry to be so unkind at this moment, but can you please tell me what is going on with Jeffrey? I'm an on-call chaplain, I don't work in the ED directly." "Oh, gosh. I'm so sorry! I just assumed you worked on this floor. My name is Charlie, and this is my wife, Diana. Our son, Jeffrey, was sitting towards the front of the bus, he always liked the front seats more than the back. When the accident happened, he took most of the impact. He's currently in surgery and they just told us they had to remove both his legs from the knee. He is a star basketball player at his middle school. He had dreams of going to college on a basketball scholarship and possibly becoming a professional player. This is going to crush him. We were hoping we could talk to you about ways to tell him when he wakes up."

Jacki was at a loss for words. This would not be an easy piece of news to share, or for Jeffrey to absorb and understand. "I'm not sure I would even know what to say at that moment, truthfully." Jacki admitted. "But we will figure it out together. How about you have one of the nurses call me when he's out of recovery and awake, and I'll come to help you break the news. This is not something a parent should do alone." Looking over at Diana, Jacki could tell this was very hard for her. Having to endure so many losses already, and now the one living child she has, has no chance of pursuing his basketball dream. Charlie nodded and she shook hands with both parents before going off to update the nurse. She was happy to see that her high school friend Sara was Jeffrey's nurse. "Hey, Sara, long time no see!" "Jacki! What a surprise! I didn't know you were the on call for ED today. That's great! Our patients love you." Jacki smiled, "that's sweet of you to say, I'm sure they love you as a nurse just as much. So, I'm assuming after surgery, Jeffrey will be going upstairs to the units. Can you write in his transfer notes to have me paged when he wakes up from anesthesia? The parents shouldn't have to go through that alone, and I want to be there to help them break the news to the poor kid whose dreams are crushed, and he doesn't even know it yet." Sara nodded solemnly. "Yeah, I just can't believe it. Like, it just goes to show you, you never know what the future holds. He was on a field trip with his classmates and

their bus was hit by a drunk trucker. What are the odds?"
Learning the details about the accident took Jacki by surprise.
"What?! I sure hope that trucker loses his job and gets charged.
He's lucky Jeffrey isn't dead! Or anyone else for that matter." Sara
nodded. "Well, another one of my patients needs me. But I just
put that in his notes. It was great to see you, Jacki. We really
should hang out sometime." Jacki made a promise to text her and
make plans, knowing that is never easy being a nurse.

Jacki decided to take the back hallway up to the SUD unit. This
unit was secretly one of Jacki's favorite assignments, because they
are in such a vulnerable space that you truly could make a world's
difference in their journey. Not that you don't make a difference
in other patients' lives, but substance abuse has always been a soft
spot for Jacki. Her friend Alisha's parents were both alcoholics
and were very abusive to her. If it wasn't for Josh's mom taking
her in, the hospice community would not have her as one of their
chaplains.

Jacki badged herself into the unit and walked up to the unit
secretary at the front desk. It was Lauryn today. "Hey there
buddy! So nice to see you today. What's you got for me today?"
"Well, well, if it isn't Miss Jacki." Lauryn said with a mock

sarcastic tone, as she handed Jacki the roster. "You have no blackouts today; all rooms are willing to be visited." "Whoa! That's a first. I'm excited! Better get to work though, see you on the way out."

Jacki walked a little further down the hall to review the list. She always held her breath each time she skimmed the list, hoping she wouldn't know anyone. Addiction is a serious journey, and one that is often misunderstood by many. If she could show these people just a few minutes at a time that someone cared, perhaps it would make a small positive difference in their long journey to sobriety and recovery.

The first few names she recognized- a few of these people were regulars who sadly just could not get any method of sobriety to work for longer than 30 days. Then she saw a name that stopped her in her tracks: Veronica Hill. 56. Alcohol Poisoning. Wants to enter a program.

While the age was slightly different for Jacki to see on this unit, it was the name that surprised her the most. Ms. Hill was one of the best elementary school teachers she had. She knew alcoholism picked no favorites, and anybody could fall victim to the addiction, but what made Ms. Hill so unique was that she was known to Jacki and her other students by a different name. Sister Veronica Ann. She was a sister of Mercy, and at the time Jacki had her as a teacher, she was one of the first religious sisters to teach in a public-school setting, due to an extreme shortage of teachers.

Jacki worked swiftly through the first few rooms, introducing herself and handing out cards to patients who did not want to talk. She knocked on Veronica's door, not knowing what to expect once she walked inside. Alcohol poisoning is not predictable and can cause many damaging side effects. Jacki did not get a verbal response when she knocked at the door, just a low mumble. She opened the door and walked inside. Veronica was alert, just going through a bout of severe withdrawal shakes. The nurse was just leaving after administering medication. Jacki stood off to the side taking in the view of one of the women she looked up to in her early years in education. A woman now barely recognizable.

Veronica realized someone else was in the room. Jacki waited until Veronica responded, before stepping closer.

"Jacki Redmond?! Is that really you? What are you doing here?"

"Hi Sr. Veronica. Yes, it's me. I'm a chaplain at this hospital now. SUD unit is on my assignment list for today. I was really surprised to find your name on my list."

Veronica looked away in shame before responding. "I know. Sisters are supposed to be holy people, not drunks like the others in the outside world." Jacki immediately sensed the hurt in her voice. "Veronica, I'm not judging you. I'm not here to judge. The demon of addiction can hit anyone. Jesus was tempted himself in the garden, why would I or anybody who follows him, expect not to face our own temptations in this life?"

"You always were so biblical, Jacki. I thought for sure you would join our order when you turned 18. Join us in teaching. But I'm glad to see you are still doing something in the spiritual field. You always did have gifts there. I just couldn't help you develop them, since you were in a public school."

They talked about random subjects for a while before the air went quiet. Jacki decided to use the silence to break the ice and determine how she could help Veronica.

"Veronica, I'm here to help you take the next steps. You're not only dealing with withdrawals, but you also had a diagnosis of alcohol poisoning. How did you get to this point?"

Veronica sat up, positioning herself as comfortably as possible before starting her saga of temptation. "Well, I could make a joke and say it's the wine at mass that gave me the bug. But that would fall short of self-control and would be a lie. So, I'll just start from the beginning. The parts of me you don't know, Jacki. I've dealt with this for a long time. I just had a way to hide it when I lived the full convent life. But, as I'm sure you've noticed, the world isn't as affordable as it used to be and even churches are having a hard time getting funding for big convents of sisters that are also going down in numbers. Our order is down to maybe 20 sisters throughout the order. When they assigned me to the school, the following year they told us we would have to find our own housing. The diocese would cover a portion of our rent, but we needed to enter the real world as simply as possible. Getting out of the sisterly routine made me depressed and vulnerable. I just started small, picking up a bottle of wine to have at dinner now and then. It spiraled out of control at some point, and I just started drinking wine coolers. Then a student's mother bought me a gift card for Christmas to the liquor store and I just fell right into it." Jacki listened with empathy as the woman she looked up to in her own childhood, now found herself feeling like a child, admitting she was powerless over alcohol. Jacki truly felt for Veronica.

"I'm so sorry, Sister Veronica, to hear of the troubles your order is facing. What happened to the sisters you were close to? Did they move too far away for you to remain close?" Veronica nodded. "Something like that. Sister Jessica decided to relocate back home in Boston to be closer to family, Sister Roselyn passed away of cancer last year. Sister Margaret is the only one I stayed in close contact with. But when I tried to confide in her that I was struggling, she disowned me. She told me those in religious life should not be as weak against these types of temptations and told me I rejected God by continually choosing this road."

Jacki felt very angry at Sister Margaret at that point. Nothing angered her more than when someone assumes that a person in the throes of addiction simply chooses that road over and over. Some do, and she sees plenty of those on this unit. But the majority are truly struggling to find a system that works. "Veronica, that is not true at all. As I said earlier, Jesus himself was tempted in the garden. Yes, there are people on this floor and all over the world who do choose to pick up a drink instead of their phone or get up and simply do something to distract them. But I can tell this is not you. You truly want to get out of these chains. But before we talk about next steps, why don't you tell me about…that night. The night that landed you here with alcohol poisoning." Veronica hesitated. Jacki could tell that that day, or evening, must have been very difficult for her.

"It was just a very hard day all around. DCYF came to the classroom for one of my students. I knew it would happen, as

I'm the one that called because she was covered in bruises. But it was still hard to see them take her with them. I felt like I betrayed her, even though I was helping her in the end. Then I found out Sister Rachael, another of our sisters, was diagnosed with cancer. She's so young and has no family in the area. I guess I just snapped. I used that gift card and paid for the rest myself and just went for it. I knew when I started shaking, I had drunk too much, so I called an ambulance. I didn't want to die. That was never my intention. I just wanted to hide all the pain and stress in something. Writing wasn't working, I prayed but I felt like God wasn't listening at that moment and just turned to something a little more instant. You must see me as someone who's so weak and unstable right now. Nothing like the teacher you had back in the day." Veronica looked away, "I failed you. And so many others. I am a horrible religious, a horrible role model." She started crying. Jacki moved closer to her and wrapped her in a hug. "Veronica, that is not true at all. In fact, I look up to you even more in that moment. You just shared that you're human. You're not perfect. You have feelings. You had to deal with a child in your class that was being severely abused by their mother, you witnessed child services removing them from your classroom, and someone you care about received a devasting diagnosis and has no support. That's a lot to go through in one day. In a perfect world, you could draw, write, journal, read, or talk to a friend and all those feelings would disappear. But the truth is, we do not live in a perfect world. We live in a broken one. You yourself are broken, and all those events broke you even more. You are still here, and you've hit your bottom point. The only way to go now is up and beyond. And that is what we will focus on. I'm going to put a referral into my buddy Sheliah, who works specifically with members of religious congregations who are struggling with addiction. She runs a treatment center in the Berkshires. It's so beautiful up there, Veronica. It's spiritually based and truly one of a kind compared to other treatment programs. Is that something you would consider?" Veronica smiled and nodded excitedly. "Yes, I had no idea something like that existed. I know lots of people go through addictions, but when you're, well, let's say a specialty genre of people, like sisters and priests and pastors, you feel so much more alone in the journey because you are viewed differently by society." Jacki nodded. "That's exactly why Sheliah created the center. She does most of the treatment plans herself. Has a few staff members, and a handful of nurses on site for medical emergencies and withdrawal observations. But otherwise comes up with everything herself. I'll reach out to her for you. I must get going and finish the rest of the unit, but I'll be back to visit. It was so nice to see you, even in this situation." Veronica sat up and gave Jacki a hug. "Thank you, Jacki! You have no idea how much these minutes together have meant to me. I always wondered what you had done with your life. I can see now that it is the perfect fit for you. I'm excited to meet with Sheliah and get my life back. Please visit me again. I know you're busy, but you took the time to help me start this journey and I would love for you to be a part of it with me." Jacki smiled. "Of course, I will visit. I'll visit you at the center, too. You were a big part of my life in my formative younger years, now this is my way of giving back to you for your inspiration." They hugged once more before Jacki turned and walked out the door. For the first time, Veronica looked alive to Jacki. Although she was naturally beautiful, Jacki saw something else in Veronica's eyes. A glimmer of hope.

Chapter 2

The rest of the SUD unit went smoothly. Jacki was getting ready to visit her last patient when her pager went off with a message from the Med/Surg nurse. Jeffrey was out of recovery and awake! She waved a quick goodbye to the front desk, mouthing that she'd be back to visit her last patient after talking with Jeffrey, said a quick prayer and raced up to Med/Surg. Charlie and Diana were at his bedside, and Jeffrey seemed to be in great spirits despite what was coming. Jacki knocked on the door with a smile.

"Well, hello! Look who's awake, about time you join the daytime crowd!" Jeffrey laughed. "You must be Jacki. My dad told me a sweet girl named Jacki was coming to visit me." Jacki smiled. "That's me. I'm not sure about the sweet part, but Jacki is correct. How are you feeling? That must have been so scary!" Jeffrey turned to Jacki. "It happened so fast; I didn't have a chance to really feel scared. I guess that's a good thing though. From what I heard the 18-wheeler ran right into my side of the bus. The next thing I know, I was in an ambulance being rushed here." Jacki let the silence hang, waiting for Jeffrey to come to terms with his accident before laying on the hardest news. Jeffrey reached that conclusion himself, turning to Jacki, and glaring at his parents. "Which, if a chaplain is here, I'm guessing there's some bad news involved. Did they find cancer or something while they were checking me out?" Diana looked away; it was too much. Charlie took his son's hand, looking to Jacki for guidance. Jacki stared into his eyes, as if she were telling him *just follow your heart, Charlie. You'll know what to say.* Charlie took a breath and began. "Jeff---I'm afraid you were injured badly in this accident. We're thankful you're still with us. But what we must tell you is going to hurt. We wanted Jacki here to help you absorb the news. And I just want to tell you, it's totally okay to feel whatever it is you're feeling. You can scream, cry, stay silent, be mad. All of it is perfectly normal in this situation." Jeffrey suddenly heard the concern in his father's voice and knew it had to be bad. "Dad, c'mon, you're scaring me!" Charlie looked over at Jacki and Diana, before continuing. "There's no easy way to say this, son. They had to remove both of your legs." Jeffrey stared at his father in disbelief. "From where? Like, my feet?" "No, son. Both legs were removed at the knee. Which means after 6 months to a year, you can qualify for prosthetics. Not everybody gets that chance." Jeffrey put his head down in disbelief. "But…how can I play basketball now? We have our big tournament coming up next weekend. The team needs me. I can't play basketball with no legs!" Jeffrey broke down crying. These were tears that offered no hope of consolation. Jeffrey simply needed to feel the shock of this news and let it take him over for a few minutes. Diana left the room, as it was just too painful for her to watch. Charlie composed himself and stayed close to his son. Suddenly, Jeffrey calmed down. What he said next shocked everyone in the room. "Move the blankets. I want to see." Diana turned around and stared in disbelief that her son wanted to see so soon. Charlie looked at him. "Are you sure? You don't have to look now." "Yes, I do. I must face this hurdle head on. This is my new life now, it doesn't matter when I'll look, so I might as well get it over with." Jacki stepped in. "You're so strong, Jeffrey. But this is a big change for you. I just want to tell you that no matter what emotion you feel when you see this---it is all normal, and most importantly, valid. They may change over time, too. These are your feelings. Your experiences. Your emotions. Don't let anybody tell you otherwise." Jeffrey nodded. "I know. There's a kid in my class that lost her arm in an accident, too. She told me how it felt when she saw her arm missing. She tells me some days she's mad, other days she's angry, some days she's sad and feels broken. I'm expecting to feel all of those at some point. But the first step is to look." Jacki was shocked. She had no idea where this strength was coming from. Not knowing what faith, if any,

Jeffrey's family followed, she could only guess it was the wisdom of his youth speaking. "Alright, let's do it then." Jacki said with a smile. She nodded for Jeffrey's parents to get on either side of him, and Jacki moved to the foot of the bed. On the count of three your parents will pull your blankets back. Are you ready?" Jeffrey hesitated, then nodded. "One…two…three." His parents slowly pulled back the blanket as Jacki watched Jeffrey look at his missing legs for the first time. She couldn't imagine what was going through his mind. Or his parents'. Jacki didn't even know what she would do if something like that happened to her.

For a while, Jeffrey had no reaction. He was just staring at what used to be his legs. His long, skinny legs that used to propel him into the air to score many slam dunks for his team. The legs that earned him the nickname 'Jeffrey the Cheetah' as he ran the fastest, allowing him to stop many scoring attempts of opponents. Suddenly, Jeffrey looked up. Jacki could tell he was feeling upset. "Well, I guess I won't be playing basketball anymore, will I? I'll really have to get my grades up if I'm going to go to college now, there won't be a basketball scholarship to fall back on." Jacki inhaled sharply at the pain in his words. "You're right, Jeffrey. Unfortunately, basketball, at least for now, is something you can no longer do. In the distant future, you could qualify for prosthetics, and they've come a long way since the early days. But it doesn't mean you can't still be part of the game. I encourage you to continue to attend your team's games. Become their biggest and loudest cheerleader. Be a source of strength for them on the court. You were a big part of that team and just because you can't play, doesn't mean you're not still a star member of that team." For the first time in a while, Jacki saw a smile on Jeffrey's face. "I know it's hard to have dreams end unexpectedly. I've been there myself. Not as traumatic as yours, but I have a dream that was taken from me, too. It's a process. And this is an unpopular opinion, but I am going to say it anyways. Laying down a dream you've wanted is not an overnight process. You don't just say 'OK, this dream isn't going to happen, so I'll just put it down and find another dream to take its place.' You pick it up now and then, you feel the sadness, the anger, you question why. You may even find yourself getting jealous of others because they have what you can't. All those reactions are normal. It's a process. I'd highly recommend finding a counselor that specializes in trauma, perhaps even a sports centered counselor is out there. Surround yourself with positive people. You'll make it through this, Jeffrey. I can tell." Jacki left her card with his parents in case Jeffrey wanted to talk, encouraged them to find a good counselor for him, and headed back to the SUD unit to finish her rounds.

"Back so soon?" The receptionist greeted her with a smile.

"I told you I didn't finish my rounds. Got a page for Jeffrey."

"Oh yeah. The star basketball player. How'd that go?"

"Better than I expected that's for sure. He seemed at peace already with it. Asked to look at his missing legs. Of course, his first comments were about basketball. I think he'll pull through though, he's strong-willed."

"Well, that's a plus. I always say, especially with physical traumas, it's mind over matter. If you have a support system and a positive mindset, you'll have less setbacks. Anyway, I'll let you get back to your roster."

Jacki only had a few people left to see. She stopped by to check on Veronica, but she was napping. She breezed through three of the patients, which were in and out visits with some of the regulars. Once again, the name staring at her next, took her by surprise.

Marc Montcalm. 45. Drug addiction. Drug of choice: Meth.

Officer Marc? Am I reading that right? I can't be. Jacki thought to herself. But it was there. In bold print black and white. The police officer at the end of her street was a drug addict. She gave herself a few seconds to compose herself before knocking on his door.

"Come in." He mumbled. Jacki could tell he was clearly coming down from a withdrawal attack. "Well, hello, Officer Marc." Jacki said cheerfully. Marc lifted his head in disbelief. "Jacki."

"I have to admit, Officer, I didn't expect to see you here."

Marc started to laugh but decided to settle for a snicker. "Yeah, I know. The do-good cop that arrests drug addicts and throws them in jail, is now an addict."

"I'm not here to judge you, Officer Marc. Addiction doesn't just choose the weak. White, well, in your case, blue collar people fall victim, too. I'm not here to judge your journey, I'm here to help you turn it around. What happened, exactly?"

Marc sat up in his bed before starting his story. "First of all, you can call me Marc. I doubt I'll ever be Officer Marc again once I get out of here. I blew that one. As for what happened, that story is too long. I've been using it for a long time, Jacki. I just hid it well. I'd go on binges when I had multiple days off in a row, stop using early enough where it would wear off before I had to go back on shift. That's why I was so tough on the addicts I arrested. I saw them in myself and couldn't get rid of the addiction. I was hard on them and threw them in jail, hoping they'd get help. I had a lot on the line if I voluntarily checked myself into treatment."

Jacki stopped herself, but ultimately decided sometimes the cold, hard truth does more than sugar coating when it comes to stubborn addicts. "Was it worth losing everything you had on the line?" Marc didn't say anything for a few minutes. Just when Jacki was beginning to question if she went too far, Marc looked at her with misty eyes. "No. No, I suppose it wasn't. I should've put everything on the line and gone to treatment. But the idea of that scared me, Jacki. I was this big, strong cop. I had an image to uphold. The little guys looked up to me. What would they think if they knew their hero police officer was really a low life drug addict?" Again, she winced at the strength of his words.

"Marc, that is not true. Just because you are a drug addict, doesn't mean you're a low life. You're a police officer. You see more than any of us would ever want to see. You have an image to portray, and you're watched closely. But you forget, you're also still human. You felt you have no other outlet than what you decided to use. You've admitted that the drug beat you, and now the only way to go is up."

Marc gave her a smirk. "Jacki, I must hand it to you. I questioned if you'd fit well as a hospital chaplain. But you do. It just flows naturally for you. You always know what to say and never judge someone's condition or situation. But seriously, can you help me? Is there something you can do? Besides the bible thump-y prayer stuff?" They both shared a laugh. "Well, I am a chaplain, so praying for you is an automatic response. But, yes, I can help you. I know someone, Kathy, who deals with first responder substance abuse. I'll reach out to her for you and set you up for admission. If you're willing, that is. I will never do something without the patient's consent."

Mark nodded. "Yes. I know I must start from the bottom, but before I can deal with any of what I must deal with, the first step is to get myself into rehab and find ways to kick this addiction to the curb. I was fortunate to avoid being arrested or thrown in jail. I called a buddy on the force, and he brought me here. If I don't get help, next time I might not be as lucky." Jacki nodded. She prayed with him, like she does with every patient she sees, and then left the unit to go and update her notes and submit her admission request to Kathy. She walked to check on Veronica, who was still sleeping, before heading to her next patient, Emma.

She had planned on visiting Patryk, but the head of the chaplaincy program took his case while Jacki was dealing with Jeffrey. Patryk ended up passing away almost instantly once the family made the decision to remove life support. After submitting her notes and Marc's admission, she braced herself for her first meeting with Emma. She said a quick prayer before knocking on Emma's door.

"Come in" she heard, in a small voice. Emma winced as she sat straighter.

"Hi, Emma. I'm Jacki. I'm one of the chaplains here. How are you feeling?"

Emma sighed. "Do you want the real answer, or the Christian answer?" Jacki smiled. "The real answer, please. I am here for you, and I want to help you the best way possible." Emma seemed shocked by her response. "Well, physically I feel like death. Oh, wait, that's because I am dying. Spiritually, which I'm sure is why you're here, I just don't understand what I am right now. I believe in God, I'm saved, I know where I'm going. I just…. don't understand why I must go in the first place. I'm 15!" Jacki nodded compassionately. "I can understand that feeling. Ovarian cancer is rare in teenagers, especially at the end stage.

But I'm not here for your physical health---the nurses and doctors are here for that. I want to know how you're feeling spiritually. I was told you specifically requested a female chaplain, so I know you're willing to talk about faith. What's on your mind?" Emma sighed. "I just... why? Ovarian cancer? At 15? Isn't that something old ladies get, after they've had a bunch of children? Originally the plan was a hysterectomy, which would mean I couldn't have children, but I'd still be alive to do all the things I've dreamed of. But, when they went in to do the surgery, they found it had spread more than they thought. Now all my dreams will die when I do. It just doesn't seem fair." Jacki thought back to her friend. "I know, Emma. I'm so sorry this is happening to you. You're so young and have so much life left to live. I am not going to give you the biblical 'God must have plans for you in heaven' talk, from my notes, it appears you get that a lot from your mom. My best friend in high school had Ovarian cancer, too. She died when she was 15. It was hard, and ovarian cancer is very painful." Emma smirked as she looked away. "Yeah. My mom is really struggling with this. She fights with my dad a lot over it. My dad has accepted it, tells me he'll miss me, but he knows where I'm going. My mom though, she's taking it hard. She screams a lot, because people have prayed for me, and I'm not getting better. She says that's against her faith. That the bible says if you pray for healing, you should receive healing." Jacki nodded. "It's a concept many people struggle with. My church calls it 'divine healing'---we believe we should pray for healing but must accept that some people just don't get healed this side of heaven. But enough about your mom, what do you want to talk about? I can't answer, unfortunately, the questions you want the most answers to, but I'm here for you." Emma smiled. "Thanks. I know you can't answer why, you're not God. And you're not medical, so I know you can't answer how much time I have left. I guess I just want to know how to deal with my mom. I am sure being a mom and watching your child suffer isn't easy. But I've never seen her so upset with her faith before. She's really struggling with the fact I'm not healed. I don't even want to see her lately because she always acts so positive and when I have a good day, she thinks I'm recovering. She just doesn't understand it."

"You're right. It's hard on a mother to watch her child die and be in pain. Do you know which hospice you're transferring to? I'm only here in the hospital, but I'm sure whatever hospice you go to, the chaplain there will be able to dig deeper into helping your mom come to terms with your condition." Emma pointed to the side table. "It's on the table over there. I can't remember the name. The chaplain's name is Alisha, though."

Jacki smiled. "Hope on the hill! I love Alisha. She's amazing. She will help you and your mom so much. Your dad, too, although he sounds like he has accepted what is coming. When do you go?" "I think later this afternoon, or tomorrow. I am excited. I haven't met Alisha yet, but I talked with her on the phone, and she sounded so young. How do you know her?"

"It's a long story. But long story short, we went to chaplaincy school together. She went to the hospice, and I decided to go the hospital route. She's got quite the story as to how she ended up becoming a hospice chaplain. I'm sure she'll share it with you, as she loves to tell everyone about her friend Gracie."

Almost immediately after Jacki shared about how she knew Alisha, there was a knock on the door and Alisha walked in. "Were your ears ringing so much you just had to come in?" Jacki teased. Alisha's eyes lit up.

"Well, well. What have we here? A chaplain turf war?" Emma giggled. "Now, now, ladies, no fighting over me." Everyone laughed. "We were just talking about you, Alisha. I was telling Emma here how amazing of a chaplain you are." Alisha rolled her eyes. "So, what else were we talking about?"

Emma chimed in "I was asking her if she could help me deal with my mom, but she explained that she only works for the hospital, and that you would be helping with that once I transferred to your facility." Alisha nodded. "Yes, Emma. Your mom is already on my radar. But tonight, we're going to transfer you over to the facility and get you settled. Do you have any questions before we leave?"

Suddenly, Emma seemed scared. "Will my parents be there?" "Yes, your dad is meeting us there. He is going to try to encourage your mom to join him, but you can't be upset with her if she decides not to go. You know how much she is struggling with this situation. Regardless of who is there, it is going to be a smooth transfer and we'll get you nice and comfortable so you can enjoy the time you have left, however long that may be, without being in pain."

Emma seemed to calm down almost instantly and seemed excited to be going. A rare thing to see in such a young lady who is going to a hospice facility. Jacki sensed she was ready and accepting, like her father, even though she still struggled with being so young. Jacki got up and said goodbye to Emma, saying she would let Alisha get to work on the transfer, when Alisha motioned for her to step outside. When they got into the hall, Jacki looked at Alisha and could see that something was wrong. "What's up,

Alisha. You look upset." "Is it that obvious? Or are you just good at reading people?" "C'mon, Alisha, you know me by now. Especially when it comes to the two of us. Now what's going on?"

"Well," Alisha began. "I don't know what your schedule is like, but is there any way you could meet Sandie at Lara's? She hasn't heard from her in a few days and is just having bad feelings. I must work with Emma, but I want Sandie to have someone with her, in case…" Her voice trailed off as she looked out the window. Jacki placed her hand on Alisha's shoulder. "I got you, girlfriend. I can take my lunch break now and do Emma's notes later. I'll head over." Alisha smiled. "Thanks, Jacki. You always have my back. I'll let mom know you're heading over."

Jacki sent Kathryn a text letting her know she had to leave for lunch early and explained she may be a little late coming back, depending on what happened at Lara's. She had most of her assignments cleared, just had to finish Emma's notes in the chart. Kathryn said she would cover the ED until she returned, if needed, and told her not to rush. Jacki typed the address into her GPS and headed over. Lara, from what Jacki could remember, was Josh's older sister. She had her share of mental health issues and gave Sandie and the family a run for their money often. It wasn't unlike her to disappear off the face of the earth for a few days, and suddenly return like nothing happened. But Jacki understood mother's intuition and appreciated that Alisha asked her to meet Sandie there for support. She prayed as she drove. Jesus, please be with me and Sandie. Let Lara be okay. But if she's not, give Sandie the strength to endure the loss of another child. I trust, if she has already gone on to be with you, that you will treat her fairly and show her your mercy and grant her peace from her demons. Amen.

Jacki pulled up right behind Sandie, who had pulled in only seconds before. It had been a while since they saw each other, and Jacki wished it was under a different circumstance. She walked up behind Sandie and put her hand on her shoulder. Sandie turned, slightly startled by the movement. "Oh, Jacki. I'm so thankful you could come with me. I don't know what to expect. She's not answering her phone, her boyfriend hasn't heard from her, she hasn't shown up for work the past two days. I normally would assume she's just disappearing like she does often, but her boyfriend said they had an argument the last time he spoke with her, and she sounded depressed then. Jacki inhaled sharply. Oh no. This doesn't sound good, Lord. Please help us through this.

"It's my pleasure. I had the time to take my lunch break early, it was perfect timing that I ran into Alisha. You ready?" Sandie hesitated as she shakily pulled Lara's apartment key from her purse. "Not really. My intuitions are not good, but God gives us strength when we need it most." Jacki walked beside Sandie as they went up the front steps. Sandie's hands were shaking so badly, Jacki had no idea how she managed to get the key into the lock. The second they opened the door, Jacki could feel an eerily cold, emptiness as they entered the apartment. "Lara?" Sandie called; Jacki echoed behind her. Nothing. They did not find her in the kitchen, or the bathroom. The living room was empty, but a piece of paper on the coffee table caught Jacki's eye. Sandie had already gone into the bedroom alone. Jacki went to check the piece of paper. Almost as soon as Jacki's eyes could make out the writing, Sandie screamed. "Lara, no. Oh, Lara why?" Shit. Jacki said to herself, running to the bedroom to console Sandie. Although she had anticipated finding a deceased Lara, the exact condition shook Jacki. Lara had started decomposing and was lying on her bed. She looked peacefully sleeping. One would have thought she'd died in her sleep, but the letter in the living room and the variety of empty pill bottles on the nightstand spoke otherwise. Sandie was trembling, inconsolable. Jacki immediately texted Alisha. Come home. Lara's gone. Overdose. She brought Sandie to the living room and sat her on the sofa before calling the police. She explained to them it was not suspicious, there was a suicide note, but they needed someone to call it so the funeral home could take the body. Alisha pulled in right behind the hearse and ran in, heading right for Sandie.

"Oh, mom. I'm so, so sorry. I'm so glad Jacki was here with you." She looked at Jacki. "What happened? Why would she do this? I know she wasn't as religious as us, but she believed." Jacki pointed to the note on the table. "According to her note, she just couldn't take it anymore. She and her boyfriend had a disagreement and she thought he was leaving her. I know that sounds like a horrible reason to end your life, but to someone with mental illness, even the littlest thing can send them into a spiral." Jacki stayed with Sandie and Alisha until the funeral director arrived, and then headed back to the hospital.

Suicide was a situation that would always haunt Jacki. Not many people knew, but Jacki struggled for years as a teenager with suicidal thoughts. She even attempted a few times, which thankfully did not work. Depression and mental illness are difficult demons to overcome. She drove back to the hospital praying for Lara's soul, as well as Sandie, Alisha, and the whole family. Poor Sandie had lost a stillborn son, her oldest son Josh recently became a Catholic priest and was sent to another state, and now her oldest daughter committed suicide. How many swords can a mother's heart take, God? Please give Sandie the strength to get through this. Keep her safe from her grief and sorrows. Surround her with the love of caring friends and family and wrap her with your loving mercy.

Jacki wiped her eyes from the tears that began falling, before going back inside the hospital. She went to see Kathryn and see if she had missed anything.

"I'm back. Did I miss anything?" Kathryn looked up. "No, not a thing. What happened with Lara?" Jacki couldn't bring herself just yet to say the words, so she just looked at Kathryn. "Oh no. Suicide?" Jacki nodded and swallowed hard. "Overdose. She left a note. Something caught my eye in the living room and Sandie had already gone on to the bedroom. She screamed and I just knew." Kathryn shook her head. "That poor woman. I remember when she lost Jacob. She took the divorce hard; I know the girls sided with their father, then Josh went into the priesthood. Now this. I don't know how she does it." Jacki shook her head. "Her faith, I guess. That must be a very strong faith. My faith is strong, but I'm not sure it would endure that much loss without questioning." Kathryn nodded in agreement. Jacki sighed. "I'm going to go hang in the ED and see if they need me. I finished Emma's transfer note in the car before I came in. If you get any floor assignments just page me." She didn't even give Kathryn a chance to answer but walked off silently. Her heart was heavy for Sandie and Alisha. So much loss. So many unanswered prayers.

Chapter 3

A few days had passed since Lara's suicide. Out of the blue, Jacki got a text from Alisha asking if they could meet for lunch. Jacki agreed and was waiting in the cafeteria for Alisha. A few minutes later, she could hear the click of Alisha's shoes. "Hi, Alisha. How are you doing? And how is Sandie?" Jacki could tell from Alisha's body language that things were not good.

"She's dealing as well as she can. She's upset right now because Josh won't do her funeral."

"WHAT? Why?" Jacki was shocked. "It's his own sister. What a beautiful honor that would be for any priest, to lead their sibling's funeral service." Alisha sighed. "Catholics believe that if someone dies by suicide, they have committed a mortal sin and thus cannot have a Catholic mass. Since Lara wasn't active in her faith, Sandie opted for a service at the funeral home with Catholic readings, but he won't even do that. Says he can't, 'in good conscience', do it." Jacki caught Alisha's signature eye roll and knew how frustrated she was. "Ugh. Sandie must be beside herself. What are you going to do?"

"I don't know. I was going to offer to do it, since chaplains can, but my manager said since she wasn't a hospice client, I'm not allowed to. I suggested we just let the funeral home pick from their 'rent-a-priest' list, but she doesn't want to do that."

"Why not? A priest is a priest."

Jacki could tell that Alisha was holding something back. She decided to let silence do its job, an old technique they both learned in chaplaincy school. It wasn't long before it did the trick.

"Well, she's Catholic. She upholds that belief, too. She's really struggling with the fact that her daughter is allegedly in hell. I've tried to talk to her about it, but she doesn't listen. She said that's how she was brought up to believe, and that's the truth. It's really causing a rift between us, Jacki. I don't know what to do with her anymore. I want to help her, to comfort her, but she just won't let go of that belief."

Jacki nodded. "Suicide is a tough topic when it comes to faith. She was also raised in a time when suicide wasn't as common an issue as it is now. Do you want me to talk to her?"

Alisha seemed surprised. "You would do that?"

"Of course, I would! If she'll let me, I'd like to do the service for her, too. Hospital chaplains have a bit more leeway in the rule department than hospice chaplains do."

"Are you free tonight? She's coming over for dinner. Perhaps if we're both there, she'll listen." Jacki agreed to join them for dinner and said goodbye to Alisha before heading back upstairs. She opted for the elevator which allowed her to bump into Sara.

"Hi Sara! How's Jeffrey doing? And how are things?"

Sara seemed overly excited to run into Jacki. They were friends in high school, but from the smile on her face, one would think they were long lost sisters.

"Jacki! What a surprise! Jeffrey left the hospital a few days ago. He went to a rehab in the lake's region. He seemed in good spirits when he left."

"That is excellent news! I think he will do well. He's got a strong spirit."

Jacki made a mental note that Sara avoided the question about herself. *I know where she works. I'll find out about her later.*

Jacki returned to the SUD unit for another day of assignments and worked swiftly through them. She was happy to see that both

Veronica and Marc had agreed to go to the treatment centers that she had suggested to them. Jacki was credentialed to offer her chaplain services outside of the hospital and did volunteer work with both centers, so she would keep an eye on their progress. She was just about to go back and check on Ronald when she got a text from Kathryn: Can you come to my office. It's nothing bad.

Jacki swallowed. Even though Kathryn had stated it was not bad news, being called to your boss's office is never simple. Maybe I'm getting transferred, she thought to herself as she made her way around the corner to Kathryn's office. She knocked on the door and heard Kathryn's voice calling her inside. "Close the door. I don't want anyone knowing about this until the proper time." That comment made Jacki wonder what it could possibly be about, but she'd find out soon enough.

Kathryn motioned for Jacki to have a seat and smiled at her. "I want to start this meeting off by commending you for your compassion and care to our patients. You are always willing to take extra cases when we're short staffed and have dealt with some difficult situations over the past year, including Jeffrey's accident. Every patient that's discharged always leaves a comment about you on their survey." Kathryn paused, before continuing. "I have decided to make you the permanent chaplain for the ED, effective this afternoon. You will always have the ED as an assignment, along with the ones that are given to you. Our ED is getting a lot more difficult patients with being upgraded to a Level B Trauma Center and I feel you are the right candidate for this permanent position. You have the balance of logic and compassion that the ED needs. Congratulations, Jacki. I feel this is a big step for you if you'll accept it."

Jacki didn't know what to think. From the time she entered the chaplaincy program, she had wanted to be placed in the ED. She took the job at Mount Mercy with the hopes of getting to that point, but never expected it would happen this soon.

"Kathryn, I don't know what to say! Being an ED chaplain has been my dream for a long time. I absolutely accept the promotion and it is my pleasure to serve the patients and staff of Mount Mercy every day. I truly love my job, despite its at times sorrowful moments."

"It shows, Jacki. And it doesn't go unnoticed. It wasn't just the patient surveys that brought this promotion to my attention. Many of your fellow staff also stopped me in the hallway, or sent me an email about your demeanor, your ability to deescalate a situation with humor, your connection with the patients, especially the youth and the elderly. You are the perfect person for this position, and I'm truly honored to have you on my staff."

Jacki got up and gave Kathryn a hug and bounced out of her office up to her next assignment---the Psychiatric unit. While Jacki truly did not have a favorite assignment besides the ED, she had a special place in her heart for the patients on the Psych floor. Even the extremely sick ones are lovely in their own ways. Jacki makes it her point at each visit to find the good in each patient she meets on that floor. She buzzed herself in and was greeted by her favorite unit secretary, Hannah.

"Good morning, Hannah! It always makes me happy to see your bright, bubbly face when I'm assigned to this floor."

Hannah turned around quickly in her chair. "JACKI! I hear congratulations are in order, Kathryn just sent out an email saying that you accepted the permanent ED Chaplain position. I'm so happy for you!" Jacki blushed. "Thanks. I honestly still can't believe it. ED chaplaincy has been my dream since I entered the field. I never expected it to happen so quickly. But speaking of, where's my assignment sheet, slacker!" Hannah giggled as she grabbed the printout from the printer. "Sorry to say you won't be here long. Most of our patients today are not in the mood for visitors. But there is one. Sue Frankland. She's a weird one."

Jacki scanned the sheet. "No real diagnosis, huh? Just extra weird and her family committed her. Stellar." Hannah giggled as Jacki walked off in the direction of Sue's room. Well, here goes nothing. This should be interesting.

Jacki knocked on the door. "Good morning, Sue. I'm Jacki, the chaplain on this unit today."

Sue turned towards the door with a big smile. Jacki was surprised to notice Sue also had Down Syndrome. That was not in her file. I guess those files are specific to mental illness diagnosis' she thought to herself.

"Hi! I'm so happy to meet you. I know, I look different. But I'm not scary, I promise." Jacki noticed that Sue suddenly looked sad. I bet her downs syndrome is a big part of why her family dumped her off. This person's not mentally insane, she's misunderstood! Sometimes the views of society made Jacki's blood boil. But she wasn't here to talk with society, she was here to talk with Sue.

"I'm not afraid of you, Sue. I know many people who have down syndrome. You're a beautiful person. I can tell. So, tell me about yourself, Sue. What would you like to talk about today?"

Sue looked so happy that someone finally wanted to be with her. It made Jacki's heart melt just looking at the pure joy on her face.

"I love Jesus! I know that's what chaplains do, is talk to people about Jesus. My family didn't love Jesus. Anytime I would try to talk about that, they would yell at me, sometimes they'd hit me, or call me crazy. I'm so sad that they don't know Jesus."

Sue's emotions were so genuine that it touched Jacki's heart.

"Is that why they brought you here, Susie? May I call you Susie?"

Sue giggled. "Susie is my nickname. All my friends at school called me Susie. When I went to school, that is. My family pulled me out of school a few months ago. They said the school didn't like me because I was too friendly. Then they brought me here. They told me this new school would be better for me. But I'm not stupid, this isn't a school, is it?"

If the saying is that one's blood is boiling, Jacki's was now at a rolling boil.

Holy Spirit, you better have one hand on my shoulder and the other tightly over my mouth, because if I ever meet Sue's family, they're going to get the come to Jesus meeting.

Jacki tried hard not to let Susie see her emotions. "No, Susie, it's not. It's not a school at all. What grade were you in?" Jacki realized she never noticed her age on the sheet until she mentioned school.

"I was in 7th Grade. My favorite subject was history. I also liked English. I had lots of friends, and we'd pray together every morning. But my parents didn't like that. They didn't think it was safe for me to bring Jesus to school. They told me the principal told them I had to leave. Yet, when I left, the principal was sad to see me go. I should've known they were lying. But they think I'm too stupid to see that."

Jacki calmed her own boiling anger and sat down next to Susie. She looked right into Susie's eyes when she spoke to her.

"We're going to get you back in school, Susie. I promise. We're going to figure this all out. You won't return to your family, but we will find you a real family. One that will love you for who you are. What your family did to you is not okay. In fact, it is illegal to remove a minor from school. You're safe here, until we can find you a new home. I'm going to contact your school and see if we can get you into some online classes to catch up, or if someone can visit with you to get you caught up on lessons you've missed. I'm so sorry this happened to you."

Susie looked so happy. "I can see my friends again! They must be so worried about me. I hope they kept our prayers going without me." Jackie smiled softly. "I'm sure they did, Susie. Even if there's only a few of you, Jesus is among all of you. I must go now, but I'll be back."

"Thank you for coming, Jacki. I'm so glad that you came to see me. I don't get any visitors. Just the nurses, and the dietary people. When Hannah told me there was a chaplain that did visits, I got so excited."

Jacki smiled, gave her a hug, and promised she'd be back once she had an update. When she closed the door behind her, she stormed to Hannah's desk to vent.

"Hannah, society really pisses me off, you know that?"

Hannah seemed surprised that Jacki was using such strong words. "OH, no. Did I miss something?" She could tell Jacki was upset.

"Sue…well, Susie now. She likes to be called Susie. She's not mentally insane. She has Down Syndrome and her family didn't like the fact she was into Jesus. They literally took her out of school, telling her they were taking her to a new school, and took her here! What asinine parent does that to their own child?"

Now even Hannah was frustrated. "What can we do? Do you know anybody that might want to take her in while we try to find something more permanent?"

"I know someone that works with the adoption agency in town. I might be able to have them come visit her and see if they can place her. If I had room at my place, I'd take her. She's such a little sweetheart. I just want to eat her up."

Jacki wrote her visitation notes, gave Hannah the names of the adoption agency worker she knew, as well as the name of the school Susie went to, and asked Hannah to call and see if they could set her up with some remote learning, and left the unit. Hannah and Jacki would get to the bottom of this insane situation. But Jacki's next assignment involved dinner at Sandie and Alisha's, and a difficult conversation.

C'mon people, gas is on the right! One thing that easily irritates Jacki is slow drivers, especially when she's in a hurry. Or when the light is green, and nobody moves. Once the traffic finally moved along, Jacki pulled onto the street Sandie lived on. She pulled into the driveway and could smell the homemade Italian wafting through the window. Sandie knew how to cook Italian the right way. She knocked on the door and let herself in. Sandie came into the living room to greet her. "Hi Jacki! So nice to see you again." She seemed calm and in good spirits, but Jacki could tell underneath that, was a grieving mother who had lost too much.

"I'm so glad Alisha invited me. Nothing beats a home cooked meal by Sandie. I wouldn't miss it for the world."

Alisha came in right after Jacki and they both sat down in the living room until dinner was ready. "So, what's new, how was your day? How's that boy you were telling me about?"

"Jeffrey was discharged to a rehab up in the lake's region. He's doing great. Veronica and Marc both went to treatment. I had the weirdest experience on the psych floor today, though."

"Why? What happened? You didn't get hurt, did you?"

Jacki snickered. "No, not at all. But there was this lady on my list, Sue. Her note didn't give me much information, other than she was dropped off by family. I had this thought she'd be some old lady with dementia but turns out she was a young middle schooler!"

Alisha sat up straight in her seat. "What? Why would a middle schooler be in the psych ward? And why would family just drop her off?"

"That's the part that's weird. And upsetting, honestly. Turns out she has down syndrome. She has a zeal for Jesus, even started a prayer group with her friends at school. Her parents didn't like it, so they made up this story, knowing she'd believe it, that the school asked her to leave and that they were taking her to another school."

"That is so messed up! So, this poor girl is missing her education and was dropped off at a psych unit when she's not even mentally ill."

Sandie was listening to the conversation from the kitchen, and popped her head in. "You know, in the 1950s and 1960s, people with down syndrome were deemed mentally incompetent. Committing them to the insane asylum was the common thing back then. It's sad to see it today, though. Her parents must have been from that generation."

Jacki nodded. "Yeah, I learned that in my psychology courses. So many common things were worthy of being committed back then. Even Menopause was worthy of being committed. Sorry, Sandie."

Everyone laughed. It was good to see Sandie laugh for once, after the week she's had. Jacki wasn't sure how to approach that subject, or even if she should approach it now or wait until after dinner. As if Sandie could read Jacki's thoughts, she let everyone know dinner was ready. The girls headed into the dining room.

"What Italian specialty did you cook up tonight, Sandie?" Jacki asked as she washed her hands and prepared to sit down.

"Lasagna. What else is there for genuine Italian comfort food? With homemade garlic bread and a side salad."

"Let me guess, cheesecake for dessert?" Alisha chimed in.

"Even better, best of both worlds, CANNOLI CHEESECAKE!" Sandie exclaimed. They all sat down together, and Jacki was surprised to see they were not saying grace before meals. Jacki cleared her throat. "Would anyone be offended if I said grace?"

Alisha looked at Sandie before nodding that it would be okay. Jacki wasn't going to push the issue, as she knew grief affected people differently.

"Jesus, thank you for the wonderful meal we are about to share tonight and the conversation that follows. May we all remain centered in you throughout the evening. We ask special blessings upon Sandie and Alisha as they grieve the loss of Lara, and as always ask your mercy upon Lara's soul, that she may rest peacefully in your loving arms."

"Amen." They all echoed together. There were a few minutes of dead silence before Sandie spoke.

"So, Jacki, you seemed like you had more to share about your day before dinner was ready. What happened to Sue? And what else happened?"

Jacki wiped a crumb from her mouth politely before replying. "Well, I reached out to one of the people I know at the adoption agency. Hopefully they'll find a good family for her that can accept her 'disability' and her zeal for Jesus. I also reached out to the school to see if she can get some remote learning going, so she can get caught up. She's a lot smarter than people think, you know."

"Oh, yes, I never believed people with down syndrome were dumb. It's sad that people assume a learning or developmental disability has anything to do with their overall ability to function. Yes, some learning disabilities are severe, but even they are not stupid. There was a gentleman at the church I grew up in who had down syndrome who became the first priest with down syndrome. It was a big deal for the community. Many orders and even the diocese itself turned him down because of his down syndrome, but he didn't give up. He gave the best sermons. Now there's even a specific order of religious sisters for women with down syndrome out in the Midwest."

Alisha chimed in, "it reminds me of the segregation issues of the 60s, we have come a long way but still have a long way to go." Jacki nodded in agreement. "There's always room for improvement." Jacki let the silence hang for a few minutes, before sharing her good news.

"Something else happened today, though," she said with a suspicious grin on her face. Sandie made it a point to look at her finger. "Well, I don't see a ring, so there's no engagement." Jacki laughed. "Definitely not! That requires a boyfriend first." Alisha didn't dare guess what it was, but instead encouraged Jacki along. "Well, we're dying over here!"

"I was made permanent chaplain in the ED!" Jacki said excitedly. "I have always dreamed of being an ED chaplain, but never imagined it would happen this soon after becoming a chaplain."

"Oh, Jacki that is so awesome! I'm so proud of you!" Sandie said. "Just the way you helped me through finding Lara, I know your compassion and warmth will be a blessing to those in the ED. They chose a great person." Alisha tossed a glance at Jacki at the mention of Lara. Jacki cleared her throat, taking this as a good opportunity to kick-start the conversation. "Speaking of…Alisha told me that Josh is choosing not to do his sister's services? That must be so hard on you."

Sandie put her fork down and paused before looking up at Jacki. She could almost instantly see tears forming in her eyes and knew Sandie would lose her composure at some point. "He won't do her services because he is bound by the rules of the faith, Jacki. The Catholic Church believes anyone who dies of suicide is condemned to hell. Yes, it is hard on me, but I believe that teaching, too."

Jacki put her fork down and gazed lovingly into Sandie's eyes. "Sandie, I didn't mean that in a negative way. But I happen to disagree with that teaching. I'm not Catholic anymore, and to be honest, that teaching is one of the reasons why I walked away."

Sandie tried not to grow defensive, but it was still detectable in her voice. "Thou shall not kill is a commandment, Jacki."

"Yes, Sandie. I know. But we are not supposed to judge others, and that includes what they were thinking at that moment of their death. How do you know, at that last breath, that Lara didn't regret taking those pills? That she suddenly realized what she'd done, and asked for God's mercy?"

Sandie sighed and thought for a moment. "I suppose we don't. But suicide is not the answer. There's help for people who are struggling."

"Sandie, you don't know what she was thinking. Period. Lara may have felt her little problems would make her a burden. Perhaps she felt you wouldn't understand. Counseling is helpful and I would never deny anyone a counselor who wants one, but just like someone battling an addiction, you can't force them to get help. And I say this lovingly, but prayer is not the answer to every heartache. Yes, praying about those things that hurt is good and sometimes does help, but it's not an instant fix. Perhaps she was afraid to talk to you because she anticipated a come to Jesus talk."

Sandie was quiet for a few minutes. Alisha sat, shell shocked, at the little cat fight that was erupting at the kitchen table. Jacki decided to be vulnerable with Sandie and share a part of herself that she wasn't even sure Alisha knew.

"Look, I simply believe that anyone who commits suicide was already living in hell. People do not just deal with a small problem and go, 'I can't do this, I'm going to kill myself'. It comes with a lot of thought, tears, and anguish. I should know because I attempted suicide many times growing up." Jacki let that hang in the air, as both Sandie and Alisha absorbed what was just shared. "Does that mean I'm going to hell, Sandie? Do you see me any differently knowing that? You're telling me you've never, ever, thought to yourself, after losing Jacob, or your divorce, that you didn't want to live anymore?"

"I thought about it, yes, but thinking about it and acting upon it are two different things. No, I do not see you differently. You failed in your attempts, and I'm thankful for that, because you do make a difference in many people's lives, but to follow through with the act of suicide is a selfish, self-centered plan, which goes against the scriptures. God creates life, and he takes it away in his own time."

"And sometimes, that time is not our time, is it, Sandie? You should know firsthand how that feels when God takes a life back without our permission. You didn't choose to lose Jacob, just like you didn't choose to lose Lara. Yes, I'll agree, it's difficult when someone we love chooses to leave us behind. But you truly do not know what was going on in Lara's head. Jesus himself was tempted to the point of sweating tears of blood. That was his temptation with agony and the evil one. His demon if you will.

Lara's, sadly, was her own mind. She is with God now, and at peace. The funeral is not for her, it is for those left behind to come together and honor and grieve. And if you'll let me, I would be honored to do the service for you, for her."

Sandie blinked back tears and cleared her throat. "Thank you, Jacki. That is very kind of you. I will accept that offer. And I'm sorry if I sounded defensive or angry with you. This is just so much to handle and understand. I want to believe in what you said that she's at peace now. But my faith says otherwise."

"Forgive me for saying this, Sandie, but is it your faith that says it, or the frail, sinful humans that claim to be the faith? No offense to Josh, or any of the other good, holy priests out there, but one thing I struggled with when I was Catholic, was how rigid and specific they were with what they taught. There was no room for human compassion, it was all 'this equals that, no questions asked.' As I said to one of my patients the other day, Jesus himself wept with Mary and Martha, when his friend Lazarus died. He KNEW he was going to raise him from the dead mere minutes later, yet he still wept. The same Jesus that wept over the death of his friend, will weep with us when we are suffering. I do not think Jesus would condemn someone to hell when they clearly already were suffering so greatly. You can have your teachings and traditions, doctrines, and all that, absolutely. But you also need to have compassion. You love the sinner, but you hate the sin. That is what Lara's memory needs right now---love. Not condemnation. He will show mercy to her, view her entire life and the good she's done, not focus only on her death. She wouldn't want you to do that, either. So, don't. It's not your fault."

Finally, all the emotions Sandie had been holding in came tumbling out. Alisha had been holding tears back herself.

"I know. I know it's not my fault. I know I didn't put the pills in her hands. But looking back, she's always struggled. I never listened to her with compassion, like you said. I only listened to reply to her. I'd tell her pray to Jesus or open her bible. That nothing can be as difficult as he went through. That wasn't being a good mother. If I was a better mother, if I didn't spend so many years struggling with my own grief over Jacob, and then the divorce, maybe…" her voice trailed off. Jacki got up off the kitchen chair and went to sit next to Sandie, enveloping her in a compassionate hug, letting her cry. After a few minutes, she pulled herself away and looked Sandie straight in the eyes, lovingly. "Sandie, that is not true at all. You were grieving for a child you loved and wanted so desperately to bring home. Your husband told you to get over it, so you hid your grief. Then you divorced, and the girls took his side. That was beyond your control, their choice, not yours. I'm not going to comment on your lack of compassion, because I feel you were as compassionate as you could be, using what worked for your own healing. As you know, grief and healing are as unique as a fingerprint for each person. What needs grieving for one person, may be simple for another. Obviously, Lara struggled with self-esteem if she felt her boyfriend was ditching her over an argument. I think she suffered for years, but never shared it with anyone. I truly believe she ended her life because she knew life with Jesus would be better than the hell that was tormenting her mind. I believe she knew Jesus and believed in him. She was just your typical young adult girl who fell away from the strict church stuff. Jesus loves all his children. Even when we walk away from him, he never walks away from us. Hold on to that, Sandie. Let his love comfort you in this pain. As you've done so many times before. Let all the bitterness, all the pain, all the anger.... let it all go to rest."

They enveloped each other in a group hug and decided to have their dessert in the living room. The mood in the room went from a feeling of division and heaviness to a light, airy feeling of remembrance. They spoke of funny moments with Lara, and Sandie's best memories of when she was first born to her teenage years. Jacki was just about to leave when her pager went off. She checked the message that came with the page:

Hi-Rise Building Fire. Mayday declared. Firefighter down. Come to ED ASAP.

Shit. Maydays are never good. Jacki looked at Sandie and Alisha and said she had to leave. "Just let me know when you want to plan the service. I meant what I said, I'd be honored to do it. I didn't know Lara well, but you and Alisha mean a lot to me."

Right before Jacki opened the door, Sandie stopped her. "Jacki, wait. Thank you so much. For sharing your own experience, your wisdom, your words, although some were hard to hear. Thank you for offering a different perspective on this situation. I am so thankful that you failed in ending your life. I'm thankful Alisha introduced us. You are a beautiful soul, Jacki. Please, be safe."

Jacki was touched by Sandie's words of love, especially coming from such a somber place. They shared one last hug and Jacki headed back to the hospital. God, please spare this firefighter's life. But if it is not your will, let his family and fellow brothers and sisters at least say goodbye. Use me in whatever way you desire in this situation. I am yours.

Chapter 4

As Jacki turned onto the road that led to the hospital, all she saw was a flood of red lights. Geez, you would think Mount Mercy was on fire! Jacki turned into the parking garage and headed straight for the ED, squeezing, and forcing herself through a thick wall of firefighters. Is anyone protecting the city, or is every firefighter imaginable at the hospital? Jacki thought to herself as she finally made her way to the front desk. The secretary sent her in Noella's direction to get information. Noella was a new nurse that Jacki had not met yet.

"Hi, I'm Jacki, the ED Chaplain. Welcome to Mount Mercy, by the way. I haven't had a chance to introduce myself yet."

Noella smiled. "Thanks. Talk about initiation, my first day off orientation and I get a firefighter mayday. Come with me, I'll fill you in on the way."

"It's just a matter of time at this point," Noella said as they walked briskly to the back of the ER, where the private rooms are. "He has third and fourth degree burns on 50% of his body. The family is saying their goodbyes, we've already administered morphine and we're at this point just letting him slip away. I must warn you, Jacki, the smell is atrocious. They cleaned him the best they could, but he's just so badly burned." Jacki had already noticed the stench, but now was preparing for it to hit her like a ton of bricks as she entered his room. "What's his name?"

"Oh, geez. That would be helpful, wouldn't it? James McClintock. You know him?"

Jacki shook her head. "Name sounds vaguely familiar. What station is he from?"

"I don't know the number, but it's the one over by the lake. This is my first experience with a firefighter. Do they always come out in droves like this? Or was he somebody important in the force?"

Jacki smiled. She spent a lot of time with the firefighters in her town. "Nope. This is normal. They're a strong band of brothers and sisters. One falls, they all come out of the woodworks to support them and their family. That's the brand-new station! I haven't been there yet."

Jacki took a breath and entered the room. She didn't know how old James was, so she did not know what to expect upon meeting his family. "Hello, I'm Jacki, the ED chaplain. I am so sorry for your situation." Suddenly her eyes caught movement in the corner, and she realized there were two young children playing with their toys.

Jacki's heart sank. God, no. Not a father, too. Losing a husband in this manner is rough enough, but a father?

Jacki approached the wife. "Is there anything I can do for you?" She looked up somberly. "Nice to meet you. My name's Jennifer. Our twins Caleb and Connor are in the corner. They're four. No, there's nothing we can do right now but wait. They've made him comfortable. I don't have anyone to watch the boys, otherwise I wouldn't have brought them. This is no place for them to be." Jacki nodded compassionately. "I understand. I'm so sorry you're going through this."

Jennifer sneered. "Well, you're probably the only one that feels that way. Everyone else says it's what I signed up for. Being a firefighter's wife. I knew there was a chance I'd end up here..." Jacki took her hands and looked Jennifer in the eyes. "But that's what love does. Love takes risks. Your love for James accepted his call to the fire department. Nobody could predict this, Jennifer. Many firefighter wives get their husbands back at the end of every shift. Others stand in the same uncomfortable shoes you are in right now. Police and military wives take the same risk. You let the love win."

Jennifer cracked a small smile as she wiped a tear from her eye. *The first of many*, Jacki thought to herself. "Do you have family?"

Jennifer looked away. "I am not from New Hampshire; my family is in Utah. Jim's family is local, but I told them not to come. I wouldn't want them to see him this way. I'd want them to remember him the way he was. Besides, his firefighter brothers and sisters are taking up all the room." Jacki nodded. "Yeah, they come out to support their brother in need. Driving in, I began to wonder if the hospital was on fire there was so many fire trucks." Jacki ministered to Jennifer for a few minutes, gave her a business card, played with the boys for a few minutes, before making her way to the seemingly never-ending line of firefighters that had thickly lined the hallway.

Jacki's buddy Mack was towards the front of the line. "Hey, Mack. I'm so sorry we're seeing each other in this situation." Mack smiled and nodded in agreement. "Nice to see you, Jacki. Thanks for coming in and talking with Jenn."

"It's my job. But you know how special you firemen are to me. I didn't know Jim, or any of the firemen at that station yet, but you all mean a lot to me, so this hits home. What happened?"

Code Mercy

"You know that big high rise on the town line? Jim was inside checking for victims on the top floor. He was almost out when a flashover happened. It was so strong it blew him right out the window. The flames got him on the way down. He looked like a flaming ball jumping out the window. It was unreal." Jacki swallowed hard and shook her head, trying to hide her emotions. "There are no words. No words I can say that can comfort Jennifer, or any of you guys. But I am here for you. What was he like?"

Mack couldn't help but break a smile. "Jim was your typical Irishman. Hilarious, loyal, dedicated. Sucked at making chili. Loved his kiddos. They weren't sure it was going to happen, but suddenly they had double the mischief when the twins were born. We'll miss his humor." Just as Mack finished his thought, the faint sound of a flat line came from the direction of James' room, followed by the grief-stricken sobs of a new widow. Jacki and Mack bowed their heads in defeat. Jacki went down the never-ending line of firefighters, apologizing to each of them for their loss. By the time she was finished, she was exhausted. And hungry. She returned to Jennifer and the boys for a few moments before heading for the stairwell.

Jacki headed to the cafeteria to get a snack after stopping by to check in with Kathryn.

"How'd that go? It sounded terrible."

Jacki nodded. "Yeah, terrible is a good word. I've never seen so many firefighters in my life. He was a young firefighter, has twin 4-year-old boys that now have no father." Kathryn just shook her head in disbelief. "How's the wife handling it?"

"Like any young widow would---terribly. She's far away from her own family and apparently gets a lot of rude comments from friends, as one of the first things she said to me was she keeps getting told she should've expected this, it's something she signed up for by marrying a firefighter."

Kathryn rolled her eyes. "Sometimes people need to use their right to remain silent more often than their right to be an idiot. That is so disrespectful. I hope his family surrounds her during these times. Balancing grief, life changing grief, and being a mom is not easy."

Jacki nodded in agreement. They talked for a few minutes longer, before Jacki headed to grab her snack. She pulled out her phone to check if she had any messages. To her surprise she had missed a few. One was from Alisha, saying they had set a date for Lara's service, which she responded to. Then she realized she had a text from a number she didn't recognize. But the message made her smile:

Hi Jacki, it's Charlie. We just wanted to thank you for all you did for Jeffrey. He is doing well and has been attending his games like you suggested. In fact, his team made it to the finals, and he asked me to reach out and invite you to come. It's this Saturday at the middle school gym at 2PM. It would mean a lot to him if you could come.

Jacki replied that she would be there and may bring a friend or two. Lara's service was Friday, and she thought Alisha and Sandie would welcome the distraction. She was headed to the stairwell when she ran into Sara.

"Sara! Hey, how are you?"

Sara seemed disheveled and at first didn't even appear to recognize Jacki. "Oh, hi. Sorry, I've been working a lot and I'm obviously on autopilot." Jacki didn't buy it. "Cut it, Sara. What's going on with you? You're not yourself at all lately. We haven't talked much, but I can still see right through you."

Sara threw her hands in the air in surrender. "You're right, Jacki. I'm sorry, I just…being an ED nurse, I try to hide my own shit from others because when I'm at work, work is my priority. But lately it's getting to be too much."

"What is? Your job?"

Sara shook her head. "No, my job is my sanity. It's the rest of my life that seems to be spiraling out of control. My boyfriend and I split up, my parents don't talk to me anymore, I've burned that bridge a long time ago. My rebellious years are catching up to me, Jacki. And I don't know if I can take much more."

Sara's choice of words sent off red flag alarms in Jacki's mind. Lara's suicide was still heavily on her mind, and she did not want Sara to fall into the same fate. She motioned to a bench in the corner of the cafeteria and encouraged Sara to join her. Once they were seated, Jacki addressed Sara's words.

"I'm worried about you, Sara. I'm sorry that you broke up with your boyfriend, but no relationship is worth risking your mental health. You need to ask for help if you're feeling that way. I'm presiding at a funeral service for a woman younger than you who ended her life, I'm not going to let that happen to you. What else is going on?"

Sara sneered. "The choices of my youth are haunting me, that's what. I know I didn't pick the best men and I know I was doing that to block the thoughts in my mind. My parents pressured me to be so perfect, and I knew I would never measure up. I know I appeared to have my shit together in high school, but it was all a show, Jacki. You don't know me. If you did, you probably wouldn't want anything to do with me, like everyone else."

"Sara, that is not true. At all. Do you really think of me as someone that would walk away from someone who had a difficult past? If that was me, I'm in the wrong field. Hospital chaplains don't just deal with the physically sick, Sara. We deal with the mentally ill, those struggling with addictions, depression, regrets, failings, faith...we don't just work with the patients either. We work with the staff, too. Which is what I'm doing right now."

Sara stared in disbelief. She had been caught making assumptions and it obviously struck a chord. "I'm sorry. It just seems everyone else sees me as this rich girl that had everything she could ever want. That I had this image I had to portray. They simply don't believe when I say I'm struggling."

"Well, I'm not everybody, am I, Sara? Please stop including me when you speak of everyone else who has wronged you. I'm your friend, and I care about you. I don't know what your spiritual upbringing is like, so I'm not going to go down that road just yet, but besides me, there is one person who will never fail you or reject you. Jesus. The only thing he ever asks of us is that we believe and accept him into our lives and try the best we can to live a good life. It's never too late, Sara."

Sara looked as if she was going to say something, but instead broke down. "I never knew Jesus, Jacki. Maybe if I did, I wouldn't be such a horrible person. My position as an Emergency Room Nurse is all I have going for me right now. I barely have enough money for bills because my past spending habits are catching up with me, my boyfriend left me, and he's not the first by any stretch. There's a part of my past that's been haunting me a lot lately and I just don't know what to do about it."

Jacki made sure to choose her words wisely, because Sara was opening her heart, and Jacki didn't want her to stop. "You are not a horrible person, Sara. You're a broken person who has been hiding for too long. Let go, Sara. It's time. What's this piece of your past that's been haunting you? Some of us are just not good at finding boyfriends. It doesn't have to haunt you, just focus on yourself and the right person will find his way. But you can't expect a man to love you if you don't love yourself first."

Sara looked into Jacki's eyes. "It's not the boyfriends that haunt me. It's a choice I made when I was with one of my former boyfriends. At times, I feel I'd be in a worse position if I hadn't done what I did, but… I'm not getting any younger, Jacki. And sometimes, it haunts me. Maybe my life would've taken off sooner because I'd have responsibility."

Jacki sensed she knew what this haunting piece of Sara's puzzle was. She didn't want to assume, though. Sara continued, "I had an abortion, Jacki. I knew there were other options, but I was selfish. I didn't want to ruin my image by being pregnant, which all the other options would have had me endure 9 months of gaining weight, being sick, and losing my figure. My parents didn't even know, I just went right away as soon as I found out and got rid of it. I bet you really think I'm a horrible person, now. Being that abortion is against your faith and all."

Jacki shook her head lovingly at Sara. She reached out and grabbed her hand, looking at her with compassion. "No, Sara. I don't think you're a horrible person. Yes, abortion is against my faith and values, but they are mine. I am not to judge others' choices without being in their shoes. You felt you had nobody to turn to for guidance, knowing your parents would have probably thrown you out of the house. You acted impulsively to get the situation taken care of---a trauma response."

"Yeah, I know all that. But now look at me. I have nothing when I could have had that precious baby. Having that baby could've gotten my head on straight and given me the motivation I needed to make my life better. And now it's looking like I won't get a second chance."

"You're still young, Sara. Anything is possible. I don't believe that baby holds anything against you. I really don't. That baby's DNA is still within you. You're connected for life, no matter how short of a time you spent together. You can't hold that against yourself. You did what you thought was right for you in that moment. The fact that you now regret your choice shows me that you cared."

Sara looked at Jacki. "Is there anything you can tell me, a book or something, on how to grieve a baby you chose to get rid of? Am I even allowed to grieve that baby, since I chose that path?" The pain in that sentence went right to Jacki's heart. "Of course you can grieve. You still love that baby, even if your choice doesn't reflect that. I would suggest naming the baby. That's what I tell patients that have an early miscarriage, where they don't know the gender of the baby. Choose a name that can be used for either gender, or just come up with a nickname for the baby. Perhaps ask Jesus to show you in a dream what that baby was."

Sara sighed. "I don't know if this is just out of exhaustion because I'm suddenly being so transparent with you, but how can

I start a relationship with Jesus? I've thought about it a few times, friends had invited me to their churches, but being a nurse that must work every other weekend, I didn't want to try something new. Another selfish act, I suppose." Jacki shook her head. "Sara, stop making yourself look worse than you really are. To others, that may sound like an excuse, as there are many nurses, doctors, medics, firefighters that work weekends. They go to church when their schedules allow and find other ways to put Jesus first on the days they can't. But my opinion is that you were not ready. The seed was planted, and you were feeling it, but it was not your time. Even if you have not given God your attention or entered a relationship with him, he has always followed you and guided you. To be honest, Sara, I'm proud of you. You may not see it, but I see growth. You had a difficult past and could have continued with that path. But, even without that precious child, you still came out of it and chose to better your life. You went to Nursing school and now you're an ED nurse at a level II Trauma Center. Mount Mercy doesn't just hire anyone, so your manager saw something in you that they wanted. Now you're here, sharing painful moments with me, and have expressed interest in letting Jesus into those areas. If you're serious about that, I'd be honored to walk that journey with you."

Sara's eyes beamed with hope and joy. "You mean that? Yes, yes, I want to start over. I can't rebuild the bridges I've burned already, but I can build my own bridge. One that Jesus writes the blueprint for. What do I have to do?"

"Well, first I'll do a special prayer with you, asking Jesus to come into your heart and your life, admitting that without him you are nothing. Then, on Sunday, if you're not working, I'll pick you up and we can do service together. On the Sunday's you're working, perhaps just find time on your lunch break to go sit in the chapel or start your shift there to give him your day. We can meet for bible studies if you wanted."

"Let's do it! Let's go to the chapel right now! I don't want to wait any longer. I've felt so lost and just didn't know where or who to turn to. I think that's why you were placed here, Jacki."

Jacki had to agree. She had applied at nearly every hospital in the immediate vicinity, and Mount Mercy was the only one that offered her a position. "God works in mysterious ways, that's for sure." They got up and made their way to the chapel, where Sara gave her life to Jesus, and started a new life. A life of purpose. A life with a destination of Eternal life, regardless of what her life map looked like before today. It was now on the right path because she chose to leave the driver's seat, and let Jesus take the wheel.

Chapter 5

After Sara's emotional moment with Jacki, it was time for Jacki to have what was sure to be another emotional meeting. Maggie had finally agreed to meet with her. Jacki had met Daniel, Ronald's son, a few weeks back. He was on a comfortable path dealing with his father's pending death, just as Janette had shared. Maggie took a while to reach out, but finally agreed to meet Jacki at the café she worked at. Jacki entered the café and waited for Maggie.

"Hi. I'm Maggie," a red-headed young lady said. "You must be Jacki."

"Yes, I am. Nice to meet you, Maggie. Thank you for meeting with me, I know this must be hard for you." Maggie sat in silence for a few moments, before speaking.

"It is hard, thank you. I know it bothers my mom a lot that my dad and I are not talking much. She just doesn't get how much it hurts that he never went to any of my school events, only Danny's. I've wanted to talk to him, but I just can't seem to find a way to do that without me being angry with him."

Jacki listened, waiting for a chance to add some wisdom. Her last line gave Jacki the entrance she needed. "Why do you feel you can't talk to him while you're angry? Your anger is a valid feeling. You're hurt, and he needs to know that."

"I don't know," Maggie said, shrugging her shoulders, "I guess I just feel like he'd try and knock it down, or tell me it was all in my head."

"Well, maybe he would do that, but he's a father. He's also at the end of his life, so he may be more willing to have that conversation. To make amends for all the times he failed you. I'm not making excuses for him by any means, Maggie, but sometimes parents do what they feel is right, without taking into consideration the impact it has on the child's wellbeing. For example, perhaps he truly felt working on your chorus concerts, or sporting events, would ultimately provide more for you than if he attended." Maggie thought for a few moments. "I guess. I mean he was at work, so it's not like he was lying to me. But why didn't he work for Danny's events? Did he feel I needed more of what his work provided than Danny?"

"I wish I had those answers, Maggie. But I don't. There's only one person who does, and that's your dad. I'd rather see you have this conversation with your father, even if it's difficult, than see you regret not saying your peace before he passes. Kidney cancer is a mean animal, it can stretch for weeks and suddenly you're gone. If I were you, I would go to see him." Maggie sat in the booth and stared at the table. Jacki could see emotions in her eyes. "I know this is hard for you, Maggie. I do. Losing a parent is never easy. But trust me, you'll feel so much better getting all of this off your chest before he's gone. I'll go with you if you want me to." Maggie looked up. "You…would do that?" "Of course I would! I don't just take the patient's side, I'm here for the family members, too, and that includes being the referee for difficult family conversations." Maggie smiled. "Can we go now? I'll go tell my manager." Jacki nodded in agreement. "I think that's a wonderful idea. Let's do it." Maggie went to tell her manager and came with her coat and keys a few minutes later. "Let's just go in my car" Jacki said, "I can drop you off when we're done. I don't mind."

They made small talk during the short drive to the hospital. Once Jacki parked, she looked over at Maggie, who had suddenly grown quiet. "You ready?" Maggie swallowed hard and shook her head. "Not entirely, but I never will be. I'm just glad you'll be with me." They went up together and knocked on the door. Jacki immediately noticed Ronald was pale and weak compared to the last visit she had with him. She was relieved that Maggie would get this off her chest, as she didn't think he had much longer.

"Hi Ronald. I brought someone to see you." Jacki said as she moved aside so Maggie could come into view. Ronald's eyes lit up instantly, and tears sprung to the surface. "Maggie! Is it really you?"

Maggie smiled and hugged her dad quickly. "Hi, dad. Yes, it's me, the wayward child."

Ronald patted his bed and gestured for his daughter to sit closer to him. "Why would you say that my sweet girl? What's going on?" Maggie looked over at Jacki and inhaled sharply, before beginning what would probably become a pile of emotions.

"I'm sorry, dad. What I'm going to say might hurt you. But I want you to listen. I haven't been to see you because I'm mad at you. You always seemed to favor Danny over me, and that hurts. You missed all my school events—every chorus concert, I'd look out from the risers and always see mom, and Danny, and other family members, but never you. When I bowled my first 300 game, you weren't there. When our bowling team won the state tournament, it was mom that ran to hug me and the girls, not you. Why was work so important when my events were happening, but for Danny's, you'd always take them off, or rearrange your schedule so you could make his events?"

Jacki could tell by the look on Ronald's face that this was the first time he had heard of these emotions. She could tell he was struggling to find the right response.

"I am sorry, Maggie. No answer I give can remove the hurt you felt. To be honest, I don't have an answer. It was not a personal thing; I can promise you that. I love you very much. I was so happy when your mom and I found out you were a girl. I would have one of each, and that made me happy, but you've always been my girl. If I had to give a lame excuse, I suppose I could just be honest and say bowling and chorus concerts didn't interest me, I felt I could be more useful if I was working and bringing in money for the household. Danny's events usually were held on weekends when working wasn't an option. I know it's a lame excuse. If I could take back those hurts from you, I would."

Maggie stared straight ahead, not daring to look her father in the eyes. Jacki could tell she was thinking of what to say next. She felt it would be another layer of pain, one she hadn't even addressed with her. "I knew it wasn't personal, I knew you loved me. You still do. But…now you're going to do it again, dad. You're not going to be there when I graduate college, you're not going to be there when I get married, or when I have my first baby. You missed out on the little things because of work, and now you'll miss out on the bigger things because…" Maggie trailed off and broke down into tears. Jacki swallowed a lump of grief in her own throat, remembering having a similar conversation with her own father before he passed. Not the same circumstances, thankfully, as her father was her biggest supporter, but she remembered this set of emotions. It had been many years since her father passed, but moments like these still brought Jacki back. All she could do in this moment was hold her breath and pray that this moment would be healing for them.

Ronald looked away. Seeing his little girl cry hit his heart in a way nothing else could. He let her cry for a few minutes, eventually raising his arms around her in a hug. "I know, baby girl, and I'm so sorry. I didn't ask for this, I would much rather be here catching up on moments with you, spending time with your mother at the lake house. Perhaps cancer is God's way of getting me back for purposely missing all those moments that meant so much to you. I can't do or say anything that can change those outcomes. But I can say that I am proud of you. I may not have been at your concerts, but whenever you were leading worship at church, I made sure to switch Sunday's if I was scheduled. I wasn't there for that 300 game, or the championship win, but you better believe I boasted loud and proud about my little girl the star anchor bowler. And when I die, and go to whatever awaits me, if I'm reunited with loved ones, you will be the first person I look down upon from above. You'll always be my little girl, Maggie. I know this took courage to come and share with me. I figured it had to be about you, when your mother asked to talk to Jacki outside. But I had no idea you were hurting so much, and I'm sorry that you felt you couldn't come to me sooner."

Maggie was visibly shaking and crying but looked up at her father. "I wanted to, daddy. But I didn't know how to have that conversation. I felt you'd tell me it was all in my head, or that it wasn't important, and I needed to just get over it. I guess my own thoughts prevented me from knowing the truth. I didn't even think about those times I led worship, and you were there. I'm so sorry. I love you, daddy."

Although Maggie was 20, this moment turned back the clock for the two of them. Jacki watched as they hugged, laughed, and wiped each other's tears. Many years' worth of pain and resentment seemed to be melting away before their eyes.

Jacki's mind trailed to Lara. How so many of her family and friends probably had things they had left unsaid, because they assumed they'd have the chance. Lara had a strained relationship with her mother since her parents' divorce. Words would forever be left unsaid. There would be no reconciliation for Lara, or Sandie, or Ed, her father. Jacki held back her own tears as she watched. Suddenly, her phone vibrated with a text message from Alisha:

Alisha: Emma passed 10 minutes ago. She went peacefully. Her parents were both with her.

Jacki: I'm so sorry for their loss. Please give them my condolences. I only met Emma for those few minutes, but she was so sweet. How is her mother doing?

Alisha: Better than we thought. Apparently, they had a talk before Emma lost consciousness. Emma's mom gave her permission to go to Jesus.

Jacki: Oh, good! One of my clients and his daughter are having that talk too. It is so heartwarming when mercy is given, and people are forgiven before a loved one passes. Thanks for letting me know. I'm about to go check on Susie, and head home. I'm thinking of you and Sandie. I will see you tomorrow. Love you, Alisha. And tell Sandie I love her, too.

Alisha: We love you too, Jacki. See you tomorrow. It's sure to be a difficult day, but with you there for us, it will be a little easier.

Jacki popped back in to say goodbye to Ronald and Maggie and headed upstairs to see Susie. Hannah was working again. "Well, hello again my bubbly friend."

"Jacki! I'm so happy to see you. Susie will be happy to see you, too."

"That's who I'm here to see. Have you heard anything from the agency?"

"Yeah, he called this morning. They have a few families that they're interviewing. He's hoping to place her soon.:"

"Good. Well, I'm going to go visit her for a bit and then head home. I'm presiding at a funeral service tomorrow, so need to finish up my message and get some sleep, it's not going to be an easy one." Hannah nodded as Jacki walked past the desk towards Susie's door. She was about to knock when something told her to just peek inside. She was doing homework! *Oh, good! The school was able to get her into remote learning classes.* She could tell how happy Susie was, being back in school. It made her mad all over again, when she thought that her parents pulled her out of school to commit her. Suddenly, Susie looked up.

"Hi, Jacki! It's so nice to see you. I'm doing homework!"

Jacki walked closer to Susie's bedside and sat down. "That's great, Susie! How do you like it?"

"I love it! It feels so good to be back in school again. I still can't see my friends, but hopefully I can go back to my old school at some point and see them."

"Well, the adoption agency is interviewing a few families who may be interested in adopting you. So, you might have to go to a new school. But I'm sure you will make new friends no matter where you go. How can anybody not like you?"

Susie smiled. "You mean I might get a new family? That's great! I would hate to leave my friends, but I'm sure you're right, I can make new friends. And you would be my friend, too, right Jacki?"

Jacki laughed. "Of course, Susie! We are friends for life now, you're stuck with me. No matter where you go, we will stay in contact. As a matter of fact, I'm going to let you in on a little secret. When I first met you and found out about your situation, I wanted so desperately to adopt you myself. But I just don't have the space." Suddenly, Susie's eyes glistened with tears. "Really, Jacki? That would have been so much fun. But I understand that space is something that would be important. I'm sure I will end up with a wonderful family. We can always do sleep overs and lunch dates!"

They both giggled. "I'm always up for a sleepover, so you have yourself a deal. I must go, I just wanted to stop in and check on my special buddy. So glad to see you are getting your normal life back, slowly but surely. Keep studying!" They shared a hug before Jacki left. Even though it was a good visit, Jacki felt heavy. Susie pulled something out of her that she didn't feel very often. Innocence, perhaps. Child-like fun and laughter. Maybe I could do it after all. She's older, she doesn't need as much play space. I'm not using my office; I could turn that into her bedroom, she thought to herself. Jacki decided she would see how the interviews went, and if they did not go well, she would broach the idea with Tim from the adoption agency.

Jacki climbed into her car and headed home. Unlike her drive in, her drive home was uninterrupted. When she arrived home, she fed her dog and made herself a protein shake and sat down with her devotional and her notes for tomorrow's service for Lara. Jacki did not know Lara personally and had never met her before. She couldn't share personal stories, other than those supplied by

Sandie and Alisha yesterday at dinner. Instead, she focused her teaching for the service on the mercy of God, and its availability to everyone. The importance of finding a supportive group to grieve with. Once her notes were finished, she climbed into bed and called her dog to jump up with her. Before she closed her eyes, she began a prayer to God: Father, please be with me tomorrow. Let your Holy Spirit speak through me and the words I have prepared. Allow me to comfort Sandie and Alisha and be a light to others. I thank you and praise you for a wonderful moment of reconciliation between Ronald and Maggie and I ask that you continue to bless their relationship as Ronald's life ends. I thank you for giving me the ability to serve your people at their scariest and sorrowful moments in the ED on a regular basis. I ask that you watch over Sandie and Alisha, Susie, Jeffrey, Veronica, and Marc. Send comfort to Emma's family during these difficult times. If it is your will for me to adopt Susie, intervene within the parent interviews that are scheduled. If a family is a good match, I will accept that it was not your will that I become Susie's mother. I give you this desire, and I know and trust that one day, somehow, you will bless me with the ability to be a mother or mother-like figure in some child's life. Amen.

Jacki turned out her light and went to sleep, knowing that tomorrow would be an emotionally difficult day.

Chapter 6

Jacki's alarm went off at 6:00. She immediately jumped out of bed as she always did, followed by her dog, who is always excited for breakfast and her morning walk. Jacki made herself some scrambled eggs and bacon. A day like today needs a healthy breakfast, she thought to herself. While eating, she did her morning devotional and reviewed her notes for Lara's service, checking one last time for any areas that needed improvement. She hoped Sandie would be pleased with her choice of words.

After her morning walk with her dog, Alisha hopped in the shower and got dressed. She chose a traditional black dress, with a light blue overcoat to off-set the black. She got into her car and headed to the funeral home. Once she arrived, she was greeted by Pete, a friend of hers from school, who left the ministry world to enter funeral directing. Whenever Jacki did a service at Pete's funeral home, she teased him for leaving ministry.

"Well, hello to you too, Jacki." Peter teased back with his mischievous grin. "Fancy meeting you here."

"Yes, we meet again. At least it's been a while. I see you're assisting with the firefighter funeral. That's going to be rough. I met with the family at the hospital."

Pete nodded somberly. "Yeah, that's going to be an 'all hands-on deck' night. We're even calling in the volunteer staff to work the entrances and exits. It's been at least 10 years since we had a funeral this big. Good thing we finished that addition. Who are you here for today?"

"I'm presiding over Lara's memorial service. I went to school with Alisha, and they were having a faith related issue finding someone to do the service, so I offered."

Pete nodded. "Suicides always complicate funerals. I'm sure you will be great. You always find the right words to comfort people in any situation."

"Thanks, Pete. That means a lot. I tease you all the time about leaving ministry for dead people, but I can see from your passion that it was the right move for you, just as moving from nursing school to ministry was the right choice for me."

After a few minutes of small talk, Pete led her to the room Lara's service would be in. Jacki was relieved to see that Lara had been cremated. Her body had already started decomposing when Sandie found her, and she really hoped that Sandie would make the choice to have her cremated, for their own healing. Sandie and Alisha came in a few minutes later, and hugged Jacki.

"Good morning. I know this is going to be a hard day for you. I just want you both to know that I'm here for you. Everyone is in the beginning, but I promise I will not walk away when the casseroles and sympathy cards end. I'm a phone call away."

Sandie forced a weak smile. "Thank you, Jacki. That means a lot to both of us. I see now, that sometimes through tragedy, you find the people who will always stand by you. Some of my friends from church have already told me they will not be attending because of Lara's manner of death. But I know that regardless of who shows and who doesn't, she is at peace and in the hands of our Father."

Jacki was happy to hear that, as the last time they saw each other, Sandie was still struggling with Lara's suicide and how her faith saw it---and her---in its aftermath.

Sandie and Alisha moved closer to Lara's urn to have some private moments with her memory. A few minutes later, a man about Sandie's age entered the chapel. She had never met

Sandie's former husband, but assumed it was him. She decided to walk over and introduce herself.

"Hello, you must be Ed. I'm so sorry for your loss. Nobody should ever bury their child."

"Hello, you must be Jacki. Sandie told me about your offering to preside over the service. That is very kind of you and is much appreciated." A young lady a few years older than Lara was close behind him. "This is our other daughter, Laura. I named the boys with J names, and Sandie chose L names for the girls." Jacki nodded and offered a smile. "My apologies for your loss. I didn't know Lara very well, but from what Sandie told me, she was a nice girl." Laura sighed. "She was nice. We were Irish twins, which is why our names are so similar sounding. We had grown apart at one point but were trying to become sisters again. I had no idea she was suffering so much. I guess we never do." Both Ed and Laura walked away to go pay their respects to Lara. Jacki was coming back from getting a drink of water when she saw Ed approaching Sandie. She wasn't sure what the relationship with Ed was like since the divorce, so decided to hide within ear shot in case things got heated.

"Hey, Sandie. How are you holding up?" Ed said sincerely. Sandie didn't respond right away, but Ed held her gently and looked her in the eyes. "Listen, I know you've had it rough, between Jacob, the divorce, and now Lara. But none of this is your fault. None of it, Sandie. I'm so sorry you've had to endure another loss. I wasn't there for you emotionally for the first one, and now this time you're the one who's struggled most with this loss, finding her." Jacki could see Sandie struggling not to lose composure. Eventually, Sandie leaned into his arms and accepted a hug. "Thank you, Ed. It means a lot, what you said. That you admitted you were not there for me in the way I needed with Jacob. I've come a long way with that, and now there's Lara's loss to face."

"You always were the woman of faith, Sand. I know how important your faith is to you. It got you through, and it will again." Ed motioned in Jacki's direction, as if he knew she was standing there. "You have Jacki and Alisha, too. They both seem to be your support system. Hang on to them." They shared a hug, and Sandie even got a hug from Laura, whom she hadn't seen since the divorce. A few minutes later, the service began. Alisha opened with a song, and then called Jacki forward.

Jacki began her speech the normal way, addressing Sandie, Alisha, Ed, and Laura by name. She opted to gleam over the fact that Joshua was not in attendance. She then began with scripture, choosing the story of Lazarus, who Jesus rose from the dead. She said that although Lara would not be raised from the dead in front of them, she would one day rise, and they would see her again. She made no mention of her suicide, but instead focused on the message of the resurrection. That those who have faith in God, and believe in him, will one day participate in that same resurrection. That no matter how far we may stray from his love, he will never abandon us. Because a father does not abandon his children. Human parents will fall short because they are human. They try their best for their children, but sometimes may not give them enough attention, or may not listen when they share, but God will always take his children back, regardless of what they've done. She closed with a prayer and a scripture from Numbers, ending by hugging each of Lara's immediate family members.

After the service, Sandie, Alisha, and Jacki went out to lunch to decompress. They decided to go to Lara's favorite restaurant in her honor. Once they were seated and ordered their drinks, Jacki broke the ice.

"It was nice to meet Ed and Laura. I overheard what he said to you, that was genuine of him."

Sandie nodded. "He does have soft spots. I think he's done a lot of healing himself. For him to mention Jacob by name was surprising."

"I'm still upset with Josh, though" Alisha said. "I get he claims he couldn't do the service, but he could at least attend and sit in the back."

"He may have been, Alisha" Sandie said defensively. "We were up front; we couldn't see everybody who was there." Jacki debated sharing the truth with Sandie and Alisha, and ultimately decided the truth was best. "I'm sorry, Sandie, but Alisha was right. I was up front where I could see everyone. I was looking for him. He wasn't there."

Sandie frowned and turned her attention to the menu to hide the sadness she felt. "I just can't believe he'd abandon his sister. Josh and Lara were always close until he entered the seminary."

"Don't think of it as abandoning her, Sandie. Just as we can't judge Lara's actions, we also can't judge Joshua's. I'm just as disappointed as you are, trust me. But now you need to focus on yourself. On healing. The ones who chose not to show up to support you because of her choices, or the fact Josh wasn't in attendance doesn't change your outcome. You still lost your daughter. The ones who were there, walked your grief with you. At least the beginning of your journey. And me and Alisha will accompany you through the rest of this painful, never-ending journey."

Sandie hugged Jacki and Alisha and they shared a few minutes of sadness, until the waitress appeared with their drinks. They then ordered their lunches, and Jacki decided to change the topic to something else.

"Are you two doing anything tomorrow afternoon?"

Sandie and Alisha looked at each other and both shook their heads. "No, not that we know of, why? What did you have in mind?"

"Well, Jeffrey's parents texted me the other day and said his team made the state middle school championship game and he invited me to come and bring as many friends as I wanted. I thought of you, knowing we'd all need something positive and uplifting after today."

"I would love that!" Sandie said excitedly. "We could make a day of it, do brunch and then head to the game." Alisha also agreed that it sounded like a good time. "Is he playing?" she asked. Sandie looked questioningly at Alisha. Jacki let out a small laugh. "Not that I know of, but I wouldn't put it past him to find a way. I guess we will just have to wait and find out."

After making plans for the next day, their lunches arrived, and they ate their lunches sharing more stories of Lara and the other children. After an exhausting, emotional morning, their afternoon ended with smiles and laughter. They went their separate ways, promising to meet up for brunch before Jeffrey's game. As Jacki drove home, she reflected on the events of the morning. A reconciliation of sorts for Sandie and Ed. A beautiful service for a young lady who struggled with mental illness. In every tragic moment, there is always something positive that comes from it. A healing, a reconciliation, or a promise to be more present to the ones we love. She continued reflecting on the hidden beauty of funerals and the opportunities they bring, as she headed home. She sensed a long walk with her dog and plenty of snuggles in her future.

The next morning, Jacki began her usual routine of breakfast and devotional time. This was her Saturday to offer her chaplain services at the Treatment Center. Although most of the clients there didn't want spiritual care, she knew Veronica would. It would be nice to see Veronica's progress. She asked Sheilagh about her often, and she said she was doing wonderful.

The drive was beautiful this time of year. Jacki pulled into her spot and went to Sheilagh's office for a brief overview of the clients that were willing to speak with spiritual care. As expected, the only one who was willing was Veronica.

Jacki went to Veronica's room and knocked on the door. "Hi, Veronica. How are you?"

Veronica was so excited to see Jacki. "Jacki! I forgot you had said you volunteered here! I am great, I'm so thankful to you for knowing about this place. Sheilagh is so great and everyone here is nice."

"I'm glad to have the connections I make. It helps so many people. And now I get to see it help you. So how are things going?"

Veronica sat up excitedly. "I have so much to share with you! The order has agreed to let me come back to teaching once I leave here. My superior was so nice and understanding."

"That's great, Veronica! I know how much you loved teaching, I'm proof of that. I told you more people are understanding when it comes to those who suffer with addictions these days. But I can understand why you were concerned. What is your favorite part about the center?"

"Oh, there's so much. Sheilagh is wonderful. The nurses are nice. Some of them come and sit with me if they're not busy with the other clients. I love the way the group meetings are run, as well as the individual sessions. And the views, you weren't kidding, Jacki! It is so beautiful up here!"

Jacki smiled. "Now you know why I volunteer here one Saturday a month. It's a beautiful area. And perfect for situations of healing."

"What about you? What's going on at the hospital? How's that little boy I heard about?"

"He's doing good. I'm going to his team's basketball game this afternoon with some friends of mine. His parents invited me to come cheer on the team in the state championships. I was made permanent ED chaplain, along with my rotations on the other units. I had a case on the psychiatric unit the other day that made me think of you."

"Are you implying that I'm crazy?" Veronica asked in her mock stern voice.

Jacki laughed. "No, not at all. But you're a teacher, so it made me think of you. This young girl was brought to the unit after being dropped off by her parents. They lied to her and took her out of her school and told her the school kicked her out and she was going to a new school. She's not crazy at all, she has down syndrome! She's the sweetest thing. Tim from the agency is trying to find a good home for her, and I was able to set up some remote learning so she can get caught up on the school she's missed."

Suddenly, Veronica looked concerned. "Oh, no. It's not Susie, is it?"

"You know her?" Jacki seemed surprised.

"I had her in school! She was one of the last students before I moved to a different school. She was the sweetest girl, and so full of passion for Jesus."

"Yep, that's Susie. In fact, that's what the parents didn't like, perhaps more than her down syndrome, was her zeal for Jesus. She started a prayer group with her school friends and the parents told her the school didn't like that. Yet, when they pulled her out, the principal tried to keep her enrolled. So disgusting."

Veronica bowed her head. "Well, I will pray for her. I hope she goes to a good home. Did you ever think of adopting her? I know how much you love kids."

"It's funny you should say that. I was thinking about that last night. Before I went to bed, I offered it to God. I said if the interviews Tim has scheduled don't work, I'll know it was meant to be. But I left it in God's hands."

They talked for a few more minutes and then Jacki got up to leave.

"I have got to get going, Veronica. But I look forward to next month when I come back. Keep up the good work. You look wonderful."

"Thank you, Jacki. I feel great. In fact, I feel better now than before I even got into alcohol. I hope you have fun at the basketball game and tell Susie Sister Veronica says hello!"

"Oh, I will!! It's such a small world. I never gave it a thought that you might've had her in school."

Jacki filled out the note log for Sheilagh and started heading back towards the place Sandie had chosen for brunch. This place originally was only open during the summer months at their beach location. They recently opened a smaller location for breakfast, lunch, and dinner. Although it's not the same location, it's the same company and it means a lot to Sandie and Alisha. They were already inside when Jacki pulled in.

"Hi, guys! You beat me!" Jacki said as she rushed into the booth.

"It wasn't a contest; we are just closer than you were. I remember it was your month to volunteer at the treatment center. How did that go?"

"It went great" Jacki said, as she scanned the menu. "As always, only one client was open to spiritual care, but it was Veronica, so it was nice to see her."

Alisha remembered Jacki had talked about the treatment center that was opened specifically for pastors, priests, and religious sisters. She thought the concept was interesting when she first heard about it.

"So, I'm guessing Veronica is a religious sister?" she asked, as she continued to scan the menu.

"Yes. Sisters of Mercy. She was one of my elementary school teachers. She was the first sister to be assigned to teach in a public school. Her order's gone through a lot of turmoil, and it just sent her in a downward spiral. She looked so good today though!"

They placed their orders and continued talking about the center, and how many people it has helped since it opened a few years ago.

"It sounds like a lovely place" Sandie said, taking a sip of her mimosa. "When it first opened, I remember thinking it would fail because there simply can't be that many religious or pastors that struggle with addictions. But I was clearly wrong and I'm so glad to hear it's doing so well."

Jacki smiled. "It is. And so is the other one my friend Kathy runs, for first responders. It's so great to see so many specialized treatment centers opening. My neighbor up the street, Marc, is at that center and he is also doing well. I stopped by to see him a few days ago."

Jacki looked over at Sandie. "So, how are you doing?"

Sandie sighed. "I'm doing as good as I can, Jacki. It's only been one day since the service, so I'm sure I have plenty more moments to come. But having this time to just relax and do something fun I think will do me good. Alisha, too. She's been working too much at the hospice house lately."

"Oh? Why's that, Alisha?" Jacki asked.

Alisha shrugged. "I don't know, I guess just to fill my mind. Plus, I love my job, so it doesn't feel extra to me. I spent a lot of time with Emma, and we had a lot of patients at once that needed daily visits. I guess it doesn't feel like I'm working 'too much' when I love what I do. It's like second nature to me."

Jacki nodded. "That's a fair assumption. I share that problem. Well, I'm glad we're all here today and get to enjoy a game." Their food came shortly after, and they enjoyed small talk while eating. Jacki went to pay the bill, but Sandie, as always, beat her. "You have to up your game if you're ever going to beat me to the check, Jacki" Sandie said with a smile. "Yeah, I can see that. You really don't have to, Sandie, but thank you."

"No thank you is needed, Jacki. It's my way of thanking you for doing such a beautiful job yesterday with Lara's service. And for helping me and Alisha through all this mess. It's the least I can do." They all headed outside. Alisha and Sandie took one car, and decided they would follow Jacki to the high school.

Once they arrived at the school, they went inside to search for Charlie, Diana, and Jeffrey. Jacki scanned the gymnasium and immediately spotted Charlie, who was flagging her down. "Hi Charlie! So nice to see you again. This is my friend Alisha, and her mom Sandie. They've had a rough week, so I decided I'd bring them to a basketball game to cheer them up."

"Jacki! I'm so glad you could make it. I know how busy that hospital keeps you. Congratulations on your promotion. News travels fast through the medical facilities. Diana went to the restroom but should be back…ah, there she is. Diana, look who's here!" Diana came over and smiled at Jacki, then turned to Alisha and Sandie. "Alisha! So nice to see you again! How are things at the hospice house?"

"Oh, gosh! I didn't even think it was our Diana when Jacki told me about Jeffrey! I'm so sorry this happened to you, Di! The house is busy. Sadly, our clients seem to be getting younger and younger as the years go by. How's Jeff doing? And where is he?" Diana and Charlie looked at each other and exchanged mischievous grins. Charlie answered. "You'll find him sooner or later, just wait. Go find your seats, the game's about to start."

Jacki scanned the bleachers. She preferred to be somewhere in the middle, versus close to the ground level. She found an empty middle bleacher to the right of the room and pointed. "Let's go there. That looks like enough room for all three of us." They got to their spots and settled in, Jacki still looking for Jeffrey. As if reading Jacki's thoughts, Alisha looked over. "You don't suppose he's playing, do you?"

"With no legs, I doubt it. But he may be in the locker room with his team, motivating them. Maybe they still introduce him as part of the team."

The school choir sang the national anthem and then the announcer began introducing the opposing team first. Suddenly, it was time to announce the Puppington Middle School Corgis. Jacki listened as they named off all the players, not hearing Jeffrey's name. Is he the mascot? Jacki wondered to herself. Just then, there was a pause, and suddenly the announcer began. "Ladies and gentlemen, please join me in giving a Puppington applause for the MVP of the team, returning to play for the first time since a terrible accident...... Jeffrey The Cheetah!!!!!!!!!!!!!!!!!!!!!!!!" Jacki, Alisha, and Sandie all looked at each other in disbelief. "What? But how..." Suddenly their eyes flew to the entrance where the other teammates came from and saw Jeffrey in a specially designed wheelchair. He used his moment in the spotlight to show his cool wheelchair spins, as the crowd cheered at the top of their lungs. Tears stung Jacki's eyes. She couldn't believe that Jeffrey had found a way to play the game he loved, despite his condition. Hearing the crowd go so wild, and even the opposing team's players cheered excitedly for his entrance. Dangit, that kid is strong.

The game was one of the best basketball games Jacki had ever been to. The first two quarters Jacki felt like she was watching a seesaw at the playground. They were neck and neck the entire time. By the fourth quarter, the Corgis were up by a substantial amount, but the Grizzlies caught up to them. It came down to the wire. Jeffrey had the ball. Jacki's breath caught in her throat as she watched. HE SCORED!!!!!!!!!! Jeffrey's team won the state championship, and he scored the winning basket!!! After the game, Jacki went running to find them, with Alisha and Sandie elbowing their way politely through the crowd to keep up with her.

"Hi Jacki! Were you surprised?"

"That's an understatement, mister. You were phenomenal! You scored the winning basket, buddy! How did that feel?"

"It felt amazing, Jacki! I had a couple bad days up at rehab. I was telling one of the nurses how upset I was I couldn't play anymore, and she told me her husband worked for a company that made wheelchairs. She told her husband about me, and he donated one that he created himself. It gives me mobility, other than being able to jump in the air. Our coach was thrilled to have me back on the team."

Jacki let her tears slide down her cheeks as she hugged Jeffrey. "I'm so happy for you, buddy. I know how important basketball is to you. Congratulations on your big championship win. It was an honor to be here to watch it. And see you play, despite your limitations." Jeffrey rolled his wheelchair over to where his mom was sitting and grabbed a gift bag.

"This is for you, Jacki. Open it!" Jacki moved over to a corner that had emptied out and opened her gift bag. It was a signed basketball! "Oh, Jeff. That is so sweet of you. I will be sure to keep it in a special place. If you make the big league, and I have no doubt that you will find a way, I can say I remember when you thought that dream was dead."

"It's because of you, Jacki. I know I surprised you that day when I saw my missing legs, with my words. But they were just words. Afterwards, it wasn't easy. But I remembered all you said that all those emotions and feelings were normal and valid, and to feel them and then let them go. I knew I had to find a way." Jeffrey's parents moved next to him, also thanking her for being there for them during those initial moments in the ED. "Your comfort and compassion meant so much to my wife and me. You kept us calm and levelheaded during a very stressful situation. You're an amazing chaplain, Jacki. We can't thank you enough."

For perhaps the first time in her career, Jacki blushed. She was not used to so many compliments. "Thank you, all of you. Chaplaincy is a job that doesn't get very much praise or compliments, so getting them means a lot. I love my job, and it's helping people in their worst and most difficult moments, that keeps me coming back every day. I will display this basketball in my office, and it will remind me on my own difficult days, the importance of never giving up." Out of the corner of her eye, Jacki noticed a camera guy and WJDD 7's sportscaster standing off to the corner, making their way closer to Jeffrey. "Well, it looks like you're about to become a TV star, too, bud. I'm going to get going and let you have your moment of stardom. Awesome job, Jeffrey. Keep in touch, I want to say I knew you when you become famous!"

Jeffrey laughed and wheeled over towards the sportscaster. Jacki shook hands with Charlie and gave Diana a hug before leaving with Sandie and Alisha.

"What a game! He really is an amazing kid" Alisha said. Sandie nodded in agreement. "I was beyond shocked when he came out with a wheelchair. Did you not know that happened, Jacki?"

"I had no clue. I suspected something when they invited me, but I thought maybe he was going to be the mascot or the announcer or something. I never imagined he'd be playing."

"And he scored the winning basket! That was an intense moment, but so awesome to watch." Jacki nodded. "I had all I could do not to cry when I heard the entire room erupt when he was announced. Even the opposing team was on their feet for him. It just goes to show you that small communities know each other and support each other through tragedy."

They said their goodbyes and headed home. Jacki decided she'd take a ride to the hospital to put Jeffrey's signed basketball in her office and catch up on some paperwork. While Jacki always did her chaplain visit notes immediately after her patient visits, sometimes she'd leave the more detailed notes for another time. As she drove, she thought of how much tragedy this community had seen in the past few weeks. Jeffrey's accident took the community by surprise. The truck driver's trial was coming up in a few months, which would bring tons of news stations to town. The firefighter's line of duty death and funeral would bring a lot of people to the area and took the community by surprise.

Jacki's phone dinged with a text message. It was Sara:

Hey, Jacki. Are you going to church tomorrow? I switched Sundays with another nurse in my unit, so I'm off tomorrow and I would love to go with you. I'm committed to this new life with Jesus. Let me know, maybe we can make a day of it, church, bible study, lunch.

Jacki waited until she was safely pulled into a parking spot before answering Sara. Absolutely! I can pick you up if you'd like. But it is Guiding Light Community Church. The address is 77 Faith Ave.

Sara: Sounds great! I'll be there. What time is the service?

Jacki: Ha, that would help, wouldn't it. Our service is at 830. I hope that's not too early for you.

Sara: No! That is perfect. I'd prefer an earlier service than a later one. I'll see you tomorrow morning. With coffee! Your usual?

Jacki laughed. Yes, nothing's changed, even after all these years. My usual Peppermint Bark with sweet cream cloud top. Iced.

Jacki ran inside and headed to her office, surprised to see Kathryn in on a Saturday.

"Kathryn, what are you doing here on a Saturday? Did the scheduled chaplain not show up?"

"You guessed it. And three guesses who that would be. First two don't count."

"Hm, let me think a second. Tracy?"

"Ding, ding! This is her third call out in less than a month. She was told to turn in her badge on Monday. I hate to impose on you to pick up some extra shifts."

"Kath- I told you, I will always pick up slack when needed. I have church with a friend tomorrow, but if you need me, I can come in when we're done."

"Sara? I knew something's been going on with her, she just seems different lately. She takes her breaks; I see her leaving the chapel a lot before her shift. You're a good friend, Jacki, to help someone find faith like that. No, I have no problem taking this weekend. You've had a rough week. And besides, you're on bereavement break until Monday, missy. What are you even doing here? And what's in the bag?"

Jacki grinned as she pulled out her autographed basketball. "We just came from Jeffrey's championship basketball game. He gave me an autographed basketball, as a thank you for helping him. His parents gave me a card with a gift card and a note inside it, too."

"Championship game? You mean the state finals? Were you just cheering his team on with him and his family?"

"NO! HE WAS PLAYING! He had a wheelchair specially made for him. It allows him to play basketball. He even scored the winning basket. It was so amazing. He'll be on the news tonight. He was talking to Brandon from WWJD when I left. I decided I wanted to put it in my office as a reminder that with God and a little imagination, anything is possible. I thought maybe I'd get some notes done while I was here."

Kathryn looked at her with a stern look. "You are to put your gift in your office and then go home. Notes are considered work and I just told you, you're off until Monday. Now scat, woman! You'll be here enough as it is starting Monday, enjoy your last night of relaxation."

Jacki laughed and held her hands up in mock surrender. "Okay, okay. I'm backing away slowly; I will deposit the basketball in my office and leave."

"Good. And don't make me follow you, woman. I know you too well. I've got the ED and floors covered in shifts, and I'm holding up the rear and filling in where I'm needed. The weekend is covered."

Jacki thanked Kathryn, put her basketball in the perfect spot in her office and then left, being sure to send Kathryn a picture of her in her car, so she knew she had left the building. As much as she wanted to help, she was glad that she had a manager that believed in staying off when scheduled to be off. Although Lara was not a direct friend or relative, her loss and service had taken its toll on Jacki. She was thankful to have tonight to rest with her dog, and tomorrow a church day with her new friend in Christ.

Chapter 7

Jacki woke the next morning and did her usual morning routine of breakfast with her dog and a morning walk. Today would be a special day. Sara was meeting her at church! Then they would spend the day together. She was sitting on the couch watching a cooking show after her morning devotional when she got another text from Jeffrey's dad:

Charlie: Hey, Jacki. Thanks again for coming to Jeffrey's game. He was so happy to see you. I hate to ask so much of you, but the trial is at the end of this month. Jeffrey is testifying and wanted to know if you would come to attend the trial. It'll be at the Puppington County Superior Court. You don't have to attend every day if you don't want to. He just wants me to ask you if you'd come and support him.

Jacki: Hi Charlie. Of course I will! I wouldn't miss it for the world. I would even be willing to speak if needed, on his behalf. It was my pleasure to attend his game, and just let me know what time and I'd be happy to go and support him during the trial.

Charlie: Thank you! It is scheduled for the 23-26th of March. Starts each day at 9AM. I doubt it will go all three days because it seems a cut and dry case to me, but they schedule it for a few days just in case.

Jacki: I'll make a note to be available those mornings. Thanks for thinking of me. Tell Jeffrey I said hello. I placed the basketball he gave me right in my office. Have a fantastic Sunday.

Texting with Jeffrey's dad took up some time, so Jacki put more water in her dog's bowl and headed to church. When she arrived, she was surprised to see Sara already there waiting in her car. Jacki pulled in next to her and knocked on the window.

"Look at you, arriving early!" Jacki said as Sara got out of the car.

"Well, I didn't want to get here late or just barely on time. I prefer to be early. Here's your coffee just the way you like it."

They walked to the entrance together and found a seat in the middle. "I always go for the middle---close enough to see the lyrics on the screen, but not directly in front." Sara looked around. "I like how this church is set up, Jacki. It's so welcoming!" Jacki's pastor, Matt, came over. "Hi Jacki. So nice to see you this morning. Who is this you brought with you?"

"This is my friend, Sara. She gave her life to Jesus a few days ago in the chapel at Mount Mercy."

"Well, welcome Sara! And praise Jesus that you were saved. I hope you enjoy today's service." Matt walked away to greet others who had come in. "Does he do that to everybody?" Sara asked. "I've never seen a pastor so outgoing before."

"Yes. That's Pastor Matt for you. Our church is based on making sure everyone feels welcomed each time they walk through those doors, regardless of if they come every week, or they're brand new or even just visiting."

The music began and Jacki was thrilled to see Sara getting into the music. After a few songs, Matt invited the congregation to be seated, and went into the message. Today's message was based on the gospel regarding the woman who had suffered for 12 years and tried every possible avenue to be healed. She found the faith to touch the garment of Jesus on his way by her, and upon touching the garment, she was healed. Matt gave a strong teaching on the story, explaining that although it is good to bring our physical burdens for healing, God does not only heal physical ailments. That we can bring him our emotional, spiritual, and mental ailments, our addictions, our failed marriages, our grief, our entire lives.

Jacki looked over at Sara and saw that Matt's words were really touching her heart. She gave all the glory to God, for that moment that allowed Jacki to be present for Sara in her moment of need, which led to her accepting salvation. Matt's voice announcing an altar call pulled her out of her thoughts.

"Today I want to do something special. The Spirit is placing upon my heart that there are people in this room who also need to reach for his garment. Perhaps you are in a failed relationship, or you are struggling with a substance addiction. Or perhaps you have been drowning under the heavy weight of depression. Struggling with a choice you've made that won't let go. Perhaps you're here today, and this message is poking at your heart to reach for Jesus today. I encourage you to come up and get prayer. Reach out to him. Tell him 'Jesus, I can't do this anymore. I'm reaching out for you, with the faith that woman had.' If this is you, please come and get prayer. We will also be opening the floor for baptisms after service. What a beautiful example of reaching for his garment, then taking his life jacket of salvation through water baptism. Don't be afraid. That woman did not care what the people around her thought of her in that moment. She was focused on Jesus. Don't let those thoughts cloud your view of reaching out to Jesus. He loves you, no matter what you've done, or what you're struggling with. He wants to help you. Reach for him today. Come to him now." Matt's altar call message phased out as the worship team began to play music. Jacki looked at Sara, who was wiping away tears. "You should go up, Sara" Jacki whispered. "It's okay. I'll go up with you." Sara nodded as she stood up and headed for the altar. Jacki stood behind her, as Sara kneeled and reached toward the altar.

"Jesus, I can't do this anymore. I'm sorry. I want you in my life." Sara cried out in sobs. "I need your healing. Please, help me!" Jacki could do nothing. She knew this was a moment between her and God. She held back tears herself as she watched her friend who had been suffering so long, finally reach out to find healing. After a few minutes, Sara stood up and went to pastor Matt. She came back with a smile on her face as they returned to their seats.

"That felt so good, Jacki! I told pastor Matt I wanted to be baptized. He told me you could do it. Would you, do it? I want you to be a part of this moment." Jacki didn't know what to say. This was a moment she would never have imagined. Not this soon in her journey, at least.

"Sara, I'm so honored. Yes! Of course I will.!"

After altar call, pastor Matt announced that a few people had come forward for baptism and the congregation was welcome to stay and watch. Sara was chosen to go first. As she walked into the pool, with Jacki behind her, pastor Matt asked her to say her name.

"Sara, do you accept Jesus as your lord and savior?"

"Yes!" Sara said excitedly.

"Do you promise to do your best to live a life pleasing to him and serving his people?"

"I do."

Jacki then quickly explained to Sara how to block her nose and prepared to baptize her friend.

"Sara, I baptize you in the name of the father, son, and holy spirit. You are forgiven by the power of his cross and made new in the image of his love."

Sara emerged from the water with a smile on her face and a glisten in her eyes that was so amazing to see. She stood up and gave Jacki the biggest hug. Neither one of them seemed to care that Sara was sopping wet, and now dripping all over Jacki's outfit. The members of the church that had remained for the baptisms cheered for Sara and welcomed her. Sara wanted to stay and watch the next person's baptism. After service, Sara thanked pastor Matt and complimented him for an amazing sermon. They dried off and headed for lunch, and then decided to go mall browsing.

"Thanks Jacki, for a wonderful day. It was an amazing service. I really feel like God wanted me there. Wanted me to hear that message and surrender my life to him completely."

"I must agree. I had no idea what the theme would be this week and that passage was perfect for you. I'm so glad you accepted him and decided to get baptized. It was so special for me to baptize you."

"Well, Jacki, you're the one that was there for me when I needed you. You're the one that encouraged me to find Him. I wanted you to be part of that. I'm so thankful that pastor Matt allows others to baptize."

"Yes, our church believes if you brought someone to church and they choose baptism, that you should be allowed to participate in that decision. Not many churches allow that, and sometimes it is met with criticism, but I'm glad we have that belief."

They said good night and Jacki decided to drop by for a visit with Susie. She wasn't working, she was visiting her new buddy, in plain clothes.

Susie was so happy to see her. "Jacki! You don't look like you're working today, what are you doing here?"

"I came to see you, silly goose! Am I only allowed to visit when I'm working?"

Susie laughed. "No. I'm happy you're here. Tim from the adoption place just left."

Jacki's heart caught in her throat. "Oh? What did he say? Did he find you a new family?"

"Yes!" Susie exclaimed. "They came to visit me with him. They are so sweet. They're Christian and very active in their church. They have two little girls, so I'll have sisters, too." Jacki didn't say anything at first but didn't want Susie to catch on that she was upset. "What are their names?"

"Chuck and Donna. Do you know them? They said they go to your church."

Jacki smiled. Knowing them, she knew Susie was going to a good home. It was what she prayed for, after all. She'd only adopt Susie if it was his will.

"I do. They are wonderful people. Their little girls will love having a big sister."

Susie looked at Jacki. "What's wrong, Jacki. You look sad. Aren't you happy that I'm going to a good family where I can be myself?" Jacki sighed. "Of course I am, Susie. I just…had started thinking about adopting you myself. I prayed to God and said if it's not his will, you'd find a good home. I guess I had hoped it would work out."

Susie looked sad for a few moments but then spoke. "Jacki, you said no matter who I ended up with, you'd still be a part of my life. It would've been fun if you were able to adopt me, but I'm sure Donna would let you take me on adventures and be part of my life still. I may be their big sister, but you'll always be mine."

Jacki smiled. "You're right, Susie. And I am happy for you. Chuck and Donna are an amazing couple. You will finally get to be yourself again, and they would support your zeal for Jesus and nurture it. I'm not going anywhere, and I promise I'll be your big sister no matter where you go in life."

They shared a hug that had Jacki wiping away a few tears. Tears of letting herself hope for a moment she'd finally feel like a mom.

But it was meant to be that Susie go with her new family. A big sister was just as influential to Susie.

As Jacki was leaving, she stopped to chat with Hannah and heard a man call her name from one of the rooms. She turned abruptly. "Marc? What happened, why are you here?"

"It's okay, Jacki. I graduated from the first level of the recovery program. Since I have no place to go, they have me here as an outpatient until they find me housing for level two." Jacki let out a sigh of relief. "Thank goodness, you scared me for a second. So, what happens in level two?"

"Well, level two is you're still observed regularly and still live with members of the treatment center community, but it's more independent. You still report daily for meetings, counseling, and so on." Jacki smiled. "I'm so proud of you, Marc. I know taking this step caused you to lose a lot---your job, your house…but you still chose to move forward with it."

"Because of you, Jacki. You showed me that sometimes, if you want to move forward in life, you must take a risk. My risk was losing my comfort zone. To be honest, if I didn't take that step, I still would have lost everything, but I probably would have lost my life on top of it. I believe this addiction would have gotten the best of me eventually if I didn't decide to take the step towards healing."

Jacki blushed. "I was just doing my job, Marc. I told you about the option that was out there, and you made the choice to take it. What else has been going on? Have you heard from anyone at the station?"

Marc smiled. "Actually, I have. My boss called me the other day. He ended up not firing me but telling me that once I'm finished with the treatment program, he has a new assignment for me. He feels my personal experience with a drug addiction would make me a great DARE officer."

"Wow! Marc, that's wonderful! You are doing extremely well. You even have a job, still!"

"I must admit, I'm kind of excited. I feel like I can relate to these troubled kids who are at risk of falling into the addiction traps and help them to find other avenues to deal with their stressors."

"I am so happy for you, Marc. I'm glad I got to see you. You have my card, please keep in touch with me. I'd love to continue to visit with you as you progress in the program."

"Thanks, Jacki. Of course, I'll let you continue to be with me on the journey. It means a lot. Hey, I heard you were the chaplain that dealt with that firefighter. How did that go?"

"That honestly was one of the hardest things I've had to deal with since becoming a chaplain here, Marc. He was so burnt."

"I didn't know him well, but from what I heard, he was well-loved. It always hurts when we lose a brother or sister. We're not the same blood, but we still support and stand by each other."

"I have some news, too. I got a promotion. I was made the ED chaplain."

Marc laughed. "Now that doesn't surprise me a bit. You're an amazing chaplain, Jacki. You have so much compassion. Best decision ever. Hey, how's that boy doing? The basketball player?"

Jacki pulled out her phone to show pictures of the game. "He is awesome! He just won his basketball championship game."

"Wait, how? I thought he lost his legs?"

"They had a special wheelchair made for him. Look at him! He scored the winning basket. It was so awesome to be there for that moment."

"Just another example of how you're the perfect person for that ED position, Jacki. Your patients are not just your patients for that day you're assigned to their unit. You keep an eye on them afterwards, you want to see their progress."

Jacki smiled. "Thanks, Marc. It's just who I am. I can't keep in contact with everybody, but there are certain people, like yourself, that become more than just patients. I want to see them through whatever obstacles they're facing."

They spoke for a few more minutes and then Jacki left and headed for home. Tomorrow she would be back at the hospital. And whenever Jacki had a few days off, her first day back was always loaded with cases. Having to pick up Tracy's share of cases meant that Jacki would be a very busy chaplain. To prepare for that, a long run with her dog and a relaxing evening at home were in order.

Chapter 8

Jacki was awoken in the middle of the night by her phone going off. She glanced at the time before answering the phone. It was only 2:30 in the morning! Well, these phone calls never end well, she thought to herself. She didn't recognize the number, either. "Hello?"

"Oh, Jacki, thank goodness you answered. It's Janette. Ronald's close to passing and is asking for you to come. I'm so sorry to wake you, but do you mind?"

"Of course not. I'll be right over as soon as I shower. Are Dan and Maggie there, too?"

"Dan's on his way, one of his friends is driving him straight here. Maggie's with me."

"I'm on my way. I'll be there as soon as I can." Jacki hung up the phone and nearly bolted to the shower. She quickly dressed and gave her dog a pat on the way out the door, carrying her work bag. Might as well just stay there and start my shift early.

Jacki headed there as quickly as she could within the speed limit, praying as she drove that Ronald would hang on until Danny got there. As she was turning into the parking garage, another car appeared to be sneaking their way through a red light. "Wait your turn, asshole." Jacki said out loud, as if the car could hear her. She found a spot right near the entrance to the walkway and went directly to his room. She knocked on the door and entered without waiting for permission, knowing they were expecting her.

"Jacki!" Maggie ran to her and hugged her. "I'm so glad you're here. It's so hard to watch him. Is he in pain? Please tell us he's not." Jacki held on to Maggie for a few minutes, before pulling her away and addressing both her and her mother.

"No. I know it looks like he's in pain, but he isn't. It hurts those who are watching more than the person who is dying. I must warn you, though. His breathing will get a lot worse as he gets closer. Sometimes it slows, and there may be large gaps between breaths. Don't be afraid of that. Just be near him, talk to him." Jacki heard a noise behind her, and everyone turned to face the doorway. A young man stood in the hall. Jacki got up to make room. "You must be Danny. I'm Jacki, the chaplain. I've been working with your family during the past few weeks. Your mom told me he was asking for me." Danny approached Jacki and shook her hand. "Nice to meet you. Thank you for coming. I'm sure if my dad asked for you to come, that you've helped a lot." He gave his mom and sister a hug and went next to his dad to let him know he was there. The next few hours Ronald went in and out of consciousness. There were moments where he could speak in small sentences and tell his wife and children he loved them, and other moments where he was completely oblivious. Jacki looked over at Maggie and noticed a look on her face she recognized as overstimulation. She walked over and whispered, "would you like to take a walk?" Maggie nodded. They walked a short length down the hall. "How are you holding up, Mag?"

"Not good. I knew it would happen, Jacki, but I didn't think it would be this soon. I had hoped our reconnection would give him some strength to rally for a while longer."

"I know. Sometimes it does, other times that person was just holding on until that reconnection was established. It's been a few weeks, so you did have more time with him than you could have. But I know it will never be enough. I'm so sorry you're losing your dad, Maggie." Maggie grabbed onto Jacki and broke down. "It's just not fair! Some kids don't even care about their parents, and they get them forever. I reconnected with my dad and now he's dying, he's leaving me again."

Jacki felt for Maggie. She lost her dad when she was a teenager. Although they had a great relationship, she, too, felt her father was leaving her when he passed away. She didn't say anything in response, just let Maggie have someone to hold her for a few moments. After a while, Maggie pulled herself away from Jacki. "Feeling better? Ready to go back?" Maggie sighed as she wiped her eyes. "Yeah. Thanks for walking with me. I just needed a minute." They went back just in time. A few minutes later, Ronald took one long breath and entered his new life, with his wife and two children by his side. Jacki went out to get the nurse to confirm his time of death and stayed with the family until the funeral home arrived to take his body. Jacki hugged everyone one last time, reminding them that her phone was open any time if they needed anything.

By the time the funeral home took Ronald away, it was 5:45. Jacki's shift technically started at 6:00, so she decided to spend a few minutes in the chapel to ground herself for what was sure to be a busy day. She clocked in at 6, and immediately went to the ED secretary to check the board. "What have we got going today, Sharyn?"

Sharyn looked up from her book at the sound of her name. "Oh, hey Jacki! Long time no see! We are slow right now. Room 4 could use you though." Jacki said thank you and went to find Sara, who was working a double today. "Hey Sara, Sharyn said room 4 could use a chaplain visit. What's up?" Sara turned around at the sound of Jacki's voice. She looked at her with compassion. "Yeah, they could use a visit. But I must warn you, it might be a trigger for you." Jacki sighed. I can't hide from it, so I might as well get used to it. "Miscarriage?" Sara nodded somberly. "Yep. 19 weeks. Mom came in because she didn't feel her move like she normally did. Did an ultrasound and baby had passed. We induced labor. She didn't want to go to L&D for obvious reasons." Jacki nodded. She remembered that feeling all too well. "Damnit. Alright, I'll go visit them and see what I can do. Thanks for the heads up, Sara." Sara nodded as she headed towards the ambulance bay to prepare for an incoming arrival. Jacki took a breath and knocked on the door. "Hi there. I'm Jacki, the chaplain for the ED. Your nurse suggested I come in and talk to you for a while. I'm so sorry." Once her contraction finished, the grieving mother looked up and smiled at Jacki. "Nice to meet you, although I wish it was under a different situation. My name is Annie, and this is my husband, David. This is our third baby. We have a boy who is 4 and a girl who is 7. Serenity would've been our tie breaker." Annie pointed to her stomach, where her already lifeless child was resting. "She still did break the tie, Annie" David interjected. "We just can't take her home like we wanted." Annie nodded as another contraction hit. It wasn't until that moment that Jacki looked up and realized her worst nightmare was coming true. That spot on the wall. It's still there. This is the same room. Not wanting to alert Annie or David that she was struggling with her own memories, she took a deep breath and focused on helping Annie with this wave of pain. "What are your other children's names?" "Mallory and Joey. We like names that end in -y's." Annie said with a short laugh. Suddenly she looked up at David and Jacki. "Uh oh, I think the baby's coming." David looked surprised. "Are you sure? Can it happen this fast?" Jacki lifted the sheet to check and sure enough saw the baby's head peeking through. "Well, apparently it can. Can you hit that red button for me?" At least that year of nursing school still comes in handy occasionally Jacki thought to herself as she ran to the counter to grab some gloves. A few minutes later, just as Sara came darting through, the baby slid right into Jacki's hands. She lifted the lifeless baby and wrapped her in a blanket and laid her in her mother's arms. The grieving parents were holding their lifeless baby when the doctor came in. "I see the delivery went well. The orderlies will be here soon to take the remains." And he began to walk out. Jacki caught sight of Annie's tear-filled eyes and knew she had to intervene. "Excuse me, doctor. What did you just say?" Dr. Lonergan turned and looked at Jacki. "I said what I said. That's not a baby, it's already dead and has no heartbeat. The orderlies will take the remains and dispose of them."

"That is not a baby?! It has a fully developed form. The gender is detectable. If that child was another week along, it would be considered a stillbirth, would you still be taking the child from its grieving parents?"

"Only because this hospital's rules say I couldn't. But regardless, that baby is dead. They have two living children, perhaps it was God's way of saying they shouldn't have more until they can afford the ones they have."

Jacki was trying hard to avoid letting this doctor know how she really felt. She opted to reprimand gently but firmly his out of line thinking. "Doctor, with all due respect you have no right to judge your patient's financial situation. This couple has just lost their child, regardless of if this baby was 20, 30, or 19 weeks, it is still their loved child, their child that has died. They deserve to have a child to bury. The values of this hospital uphold that life starts at conception and in the case of a premature death during pregnancy, the parents are allowed to have their child's remains if they wish for their own private funeral. And you may be willing to ignore that fact, but I am not. You dispose of that child; I will find where you put it and make sure that David and Annie are given their precious daughter." Suddenly, Jacki realized there was movement behind her. Kathryn and the ED Director, Tom, approached them. "Is there a problem here, Jacki?" Kathryn asked.

"Morning, Kathryn, Tom." Jacki said in a friendly tone, hoping it would calm her down. "As a matter of fact, there is. Doctor charming here is refusing to give the grieving parents in room 4 their deceased daughter's body. He also made a remark about their financial situation, saying perhaps God allowed them to lose their daughter so they could focus on their two other children."

Tom's eyes grew wide, and you could almost see smoke coming out of his ears. "Alan, you know the values of this hospital are based on the Christian teachings of life in all its phases. I am shocked to hear of this activity."

"Well, we're already not going to get any money for her care since they're on the state insurance. Don't you think it's irritating that these simple-minded people can just take advantage of the hospitals by having children without paying for them properly? I didn't ask to be placed in a hospital filled with poor people on state insurance as patients. My medical program sent me here."

"Well, on that note, you are to clean out your locker and hand in your badge. This is not your first negative experience with a patient, Alan. Last week you ignored a terminally ill patient's DNR, and the week before you nearly killed a patient because you did not check her allergy bracelet before administering medication. If you are becoming a doctor because you want to serve rich patients, then perhaps you should relocate to a wealthier state. I will make sure your medical school dean is aware of these three instances and request he transfer you, or perhaps even terminate your education, immediately. Mount Mercy does not tolerate self-centered doctors. Goodbye Alan."

Alan slammed his badge on the nurse's desk and stormed off. Tom watched him leave before turning his attention back to Jacki. "And you, Jacki. I commend you strongly for speaking up and advocating for that family. I also hear you were the midwife on duty in there, congratulations." Jacki smiled. "Yeah, it was a quick moment in time I wasn't expecting. But I was happy I could speak up for them." Jacki was headed back to the room when Kathryn pulled her aside. "Good job, Jacki. You kept your cool but still made your point heard. I know this situation must bring back memories for you." Jacki looked away for a second. "Same room, you know," she said. "Same exact room. Only she was a few weeks behind me." Kathryn nodded. "I know. When

Sara told me you had gone in, I held my breath. But I suppose working here you won't be able to hide from it much longer. Good job, Jacki. Feel free to take some time to cool off if you need to, before going to another unit." Jacki smiled lightly. "Thanks, Kath. I probably will go take a walk. But first, I'm going to go visit Annie and David and little Serenity."

Jacki walked back in. David and Annie looked up at her when she walked through the door. Jacki could still see the fear in her eyes. "It's okay Annie, nobody's going to take your angel away from you. Just the funeral home you choose when you're ready to do that." The fear melted from both of their faces. "Oh, thank you Jacki. And thank you for speaking up for us. We couldn't believe what that doctor was saying about us. We could hear you standing up for us."

Jacki nodded in agreement. "Well, you know what they say, you can learn how to be a doctor in the scientific sense from textbooks, but no textbook can give you bedside manner. It's either in you or it's not. Clearly, he only has bedside manner for wealthy people. He won't be with this hospital any longer." Jacki walked over to where Annie was sitting. "You did, good, Annie."

"Well, it is my third, after all. I suppose the body knows no difference; labor is labor. And mine seem to go quickly. You were great yourself! I didn't know chaplains were trained to deliver babies." Jacki laughed. "Yeah, it's not exactly in our contract, but luckily, I took a year of nursing school before I decided it wasn't my perfect fit. On occasion, I get to use those skills. So, what is miss Serenity's middle name?" Annie and David looked at each other. "Well, as a matter of fact, we didn't have one chosen yet. But I think Serenity Jacquelynne sounds perfect, after the lovely lady who delivered her and advocated for her." Jacki was stunned. She held her breath, hoping that she could find words without falling apart. "Oh, Annie. That is so kind of you. If you're sure that is the middle name you want for her, I'd be honored. May I ask a personal question?"

"Of course, anything."

"Do you believe? Do you want Serenity baptized? Chaplains can do infant baptisms if desired." David and Annie looked at each other, before Annie responded. "Oh, Jacki, would you? We just moved here not too long ago and haven't joined a church yet. Our faith believes baptism should be done when you're a little older than a newborn, but Serenity won't get the chance to make that choice herself."

"It would be my pleasure." Jacki went to the chapel and grabbed some holy water, and baptized Serenity with both her parents, and Sara came in to act as the witness. After the baptism was completed, Sara printed out an emergency certificate of baptism for the parents. Jacki hugged Annie and David goodbye and gave them her card, encouraging them to reach out to her whenever they needed. Sara followed Jacki out of the room. "You okay?" Jacki sighed. "Surprisingly, yes. I can't hide from it forever. I knew taking the ED position I'd be bound to be in that room again at some point. But Kathryn said I could take some time before going to my assigned units, so I'm just going to go take a walk and decompress. Page me if you need me."

Sara gave Jacki a hug. "Will do. You know where I am if you need someone. You were there for me; I can be there for you. I must go work on their discharge paperwork in between cleaning rooms. We can't find Ana anywhere."

"Ana?! That's odd. Maybe she's tied up on another unit." Sara nodded. "Possibly. I know they were short the last couple weeks, so she might be working a different floor first."

Jacki left the ED and headed up the stairs. She wandered on auto pilot and found herself headed for the nursery. Mount Mercy was one of the few hospitals that still had the old-fashioned window nursery that people could stand at the window and see all the babies. Jacki stood there, emotionless, just looking blankly into the window. She cracked a small smile as one of the babies seemed to be pointing toward her. She placed her forehead gently against the window and let her mind wander. She never noticed the small pool of tears that had started collecting on the windowpane and never heard anybody approaching her. A touch on her shoulder made her jump. "Hey, sorry to startle you. I just wanted to check on you, girlfriend." Jacki turned, catching her heart as it leaped into her throat. "Trina! I forgot you worked up here." Jacki sniffled and tried to regain her composure. Trina placed her hand on Jacki's shoulder and gently stood next to her. "Are you okay? You're never up here." Jacki took a shaky breath before answering. "Yeah, you know. Sometimes you must visit your sorrows. Pick them up, look at them, feel them, spend time with the memory and then put it back on the shelf. I had to minister to a couple that had a late term miscarriage. She was just a week shy of the 20-week mark. Little girl. She was in the same room that I was in when I lost my baby. Just brought up a lot of memories. Decided to come up here and take out that wound, sit with it for a while." Trina nodded compassionately. "Understandable. I'm sure that was difficult for you. I won't keep you, just wanted to check on you. I could see the tears

falling as I turned the corner." Jacki sniffled and tried to laugh.
"Yeah, when I go to that place, the tears fall easily. It doesn't
matter how many years, when you go back to that pain, it'll always
be there." Trina gave Jacki a quick hug and went off on her way
back to her unit. Jacki stayed a few more minutes, talking to her
own daughter in her mind. She took a deep breath and wiped
away her tears before walking away.

As she headed towards the main hallway, she suddenly realized
that the sounds near the roof entrance seemed louder. Why
would that door be opened? She thought to herself as she walked
cautiously toward the door. Sure enough, it was open a little bit.
Jacki suddenly felt lured to investigate. As she prayed to God for
protection, she carefully followed the stairs. When she got to the
roof, she couldn't believe what she saw. Oh God! Ana! OK,
Jacki keep calm. You can't scare her or else she may go over. She
stayed far back, out of sight, and quietly pulled out her phone.
She added Tom, Kathryn and Sara's number to a group text and
wrote: Code Mercy. Ana from environmental is on the roof. Send
help! But please come quietly, she is very close to the edge.

While waiting for help, Jacki slowly and quietly inched closer to
Ana. She must have sensed that someone was there, as she slowly

turned from looking over the rooftop. "Jacki- don't try and save me. This is the only answer to the demons in my mind." Ana seemed to turn her attention back towards looking over the rooftop and moved closer to the edge. "Ana! You know that's not true! Please, back away from the edge. Just a little bit." Ana started to move away, and changed her mind, instead inching even closer. Jacki couldn't wait for anyone else to arrive. Remember your training, act swiftly and aim for the waist, wrapping them like a hug, and pull away gently. Jacki quietly lunged toward Ana, wrapping her in a safety hug and pulling her to safety just as Tom and Kathryn barged through the door with ED nurses in tow. Ana fought for a few minutes before giving up and climbing onto the stretcher. The next set of eyes Ana met were Tom's. He spoke compassionately to her and promised her they'd check her out and get her the help she needed. Jacki was still trying to calm her breathing when Kathryn walked over to her.

"Hey, I said take a walk and destress, I didn't say find more stress." Jacki let out a laugh. "I did, believe it or not. I went to the place I always do when I need to visit that moment in my own life. On my way back, I realized the noise from the staircase sounded louder, so went to investigate." Jacki's voice trailed off; she didn't feel the need to continue.

"Well, I'm glad you did, Jacki. If you had ignored the increased sounds, or not even noticed them, we could have a serious tragedy on our hands. You saved Ana. Thank you."

"All in a day's work for a chaplain, I guess. My pleasure." Jacki walked slowly away when Kathryn suddenly stopped her. "Hey, Jacki? What made you think of the saying Code Mercy in your text?" Jacki paused. "I don't know. It just came to me. Kind of like when you're on the floor and someone codes. I thought Mercy worked well because it's the hospital name, but also, suicide and mercy go together." Kathryn nodded. "I think that is going to be a new code to implement. Whenever an attempted suicide, or overdose comes in, we will use code mercy. Most definitely when it's a staff member, too." Jacki smiled. "Glad I could be of assistance with my quick thinking, in both examples. I'm going to go grab my assignment sheets before I get into more trouble."

Kathryn laughed. "Yeah, good idea. You've already delivered a baby, saved someone from jumping to their death…what's next? On second thought, don't answer that."

Jacki left the rooftop and went back towards her office to check what units she was assigned to for the rest of her shift. She glanced at the clock. Gee whiz, it's only 11? It feels like it should be close to the end of the day. Well, I knew it would be busy. She made a mental note to visit Ana later, and went to work on her remaining assignments, hoping and praying for no more mishaps and unexpected turn of event scenarios.

Chapter 9

Jacki read through her assignments, organizing them by level of importance. She had both the SUD and Psychiatric units today, which meant she'd get to visit Ana. She always had the ED now, which always ran the chance of ruining her order of visits. She had a few Palliative Care visits on her list today as well, but it was the one at the end that once again gave her a lump in her throat. L&D: Bethany Lacroix. Husband Brandon. Stillborn daughter, born at full-term overnight. Wants baby baptized and needs spiritual comfort and direction.

God, please give me the strength to help this grieving family. Help me to comfort them in their difficult, painful loss, as you have helped me with my own. You are testing my healing with these difficult patient experiences. Jacki decided to save that for her last visit of the day, as she knew it would be difficult.

Deciding to start on the psychiatric floor, she was surprised to run into her favorite patient, Susie, who was being discharged to her new home. "JACKI!" Susie exclaimed, as she ran to hug her. "I'm so glad I got to see you before I went to my new family." Jacki returned her hug and held her tight for a few moments, trying not to lose her composure. "I'm so glad I decided to come here first! You must be so excited to go home and play with your new sisters." She looked at Donna and waved. "Hi, Donna- thanks so much for adopting Susie. She's meant a lot to me as I got to know her in the past few weeks, and I'm happy that she is going with someone I know. I couldn't have chosen a better family." Donna came over and gave Jacki a hug after Susie had run on ahead. "Thank you, Jacki. It was our pleasure to answer God's call to add another girl to our family. But I know this is hard for you. Tim had told me you were debating adopting her yourself. I know how much you miss your little angel and how deeply you've wanted to be someone's mother." Jacki looked away quickly before replying. "I was thinking about it, but the truth is, I don't think I could've done it. I'm sure I would've made it work, but she's better off with a real family. Siblings to play with, two parents full of love. I can't give her any of that. And I have plans to spend time with her often, if that's okay with you, of course. I can't be her mom, but there's no rule that says I can't be her big sister." Donna patted her on the shoulder. "Of course that's okay. We will encourage both of you to do things together often. You saved her, in a sense, Jacki. We're just ensuring that she remains on a good path of love. You're so strong, Jacki. I honestly don't know how you do it." *I wasn't given much of a choice,* Jacki thought to herself. Instead of saying it out loud, she simply smiled at Donna and waved goodbye to Susie, promising to make plans soon to do something fun. Hannah wasn't on yet; it was some other woman she hadn't seen before. She did not appear very friendly, so Jacki just got started going through her patients. As was typical for this floor, not many patients wanted a spiritual care visit. The nurse was just finishing up with Ana when she made it to the last room. New admits were given the rooms farthest from the desk, so that their sensory reactions would not become overstimulated. "Is she okay for visitors?" Jacki asked the nurse on her way out. Jacki noticed that the name said *Holly*. Holly looked at Jacki and noticed her badge. "Regular visitors, not yet. But hospital chaplains, absolutely" she said with a smile. Jacki nodded with a smile and knocked on the door gently. "Ana? It's Jacki." Jacki inched the door open and found Ana just lying in her bed, staring blankly at the other side of the room. A typical reaction for someone who had attempted suicide and failed. Jacki moved closer, not wanting to scare her. "Ana?"

"I heard you." Ana said softly. "But if you're here to give me the Jesus is upset with me talk, I'm not interested." Jacki let out a sigh and sat in a chair next to Ana. She was beginning to feel like a broken record.

"No, Ana. Jesus is not upset with you. Jesus suffered, too. I know you know your bible stories, so I'm not going to list all of them. I'm so glad I was there, Ana."

Ana sighed. "Me, too. I mean, I'm still upset that I didn't follow through, but I know. Or at least hope that someday I'll be thankful I'm still here. How'd you even know I was up there; do you have a sixth sense or something?"

Jacki let out a small laugh. "I guess you could call it that. I went up to the nursery window to have a moment after a tough case in the ED and could hear the noises from the hallway louder than usual. That's when I realized the door was slightly open, and I just decided to follow it." Jacki paused before asking the next question. "Ana, you don't have to tell me if you don't want to, but you know I'm going to ask. Why? What were you thinking? What's going on that would make you think about ending your life in such a tragic way?" Ana looked away, trying to find the right words to answer that question. "I don't know, Jacki. I really don't. I can't describe it. I've just felt so down lately. The past few weeks, it's gotten worse and heavier each day. I just couldn't take it anymore. I came in early so nobody would notice." "Has anything been going on in your life that would make you want to hurt yourself like that? I know you're divorced, but I thought that was years ago." Ana nodded. "It has been 10 years. It's not that.

The kids are doing great. My baby left for college, so I suppose you could say it's that empty nester syndrome, but we talk almost every weekend." As Jacki was listening, something dawned on her. Kids…youngest just entered college, puts her about 18 I wonder…. Jacki's thoughts trailed off.

"Ana, can I ask you a personal question?"

"I suppose. What's on your mind?"

"Have you stopped your periods yet?"

Ana was quiet, as if she were deep in thought. Suddenly, it was obvious the thought had never occurred to her. "As a matter of fact, the last one I had was about six months ago! Do you really think it's just menopause?"

"I will let your charge nurse know to investigate it, perhaps have an OB consult come in. Menopause and hormones can make people do things that are not normal. There is also a rare disorder, PMDD, that can cause your hormones to go completely out of whack, which has been known to cause suicidal or even homicidal thoughts in some women. It's more common in younger women, but can hit during the menopausal stages, too. I'm not a genetics counselor or anything but being that you had no outside factors that would point you in that direction, I'm betting it's the hormones that are to blame." Jacki smiled at Ana. She could tell that Ana suddenly relaxed. "Thank you, Jacki. You made me feel so much better. I was so worried I had something seriously wrong with me. It's not like me, you know that. I love my job, my kids, my faith…to end it all, and in such a violent manner, would not be me at all." Jacki nodded in agreement. "I knew that, Ana. When I saw you up there, I knew it wasn't the real you. The Ana I knew wouldn't end her life and leave all her precious children without a mother. That's why I truly believe the Holy Spirit nudged me to explore. To find you so I could save you from making that mistake."

They talked for a few more minutes, and then Ana said she was exhausted and wanted to get some sleep. Jacki nodded in agreement and went to update the charge nurse prior to heading to the SUD unit. By the time she was heading out, Hannah had come in for her shift. "Hey, sunshine!" Jacki said with a smile. "I was just headed out. Saw our prized patient went home to her new family, caught her as I was coming in."

"Oh good! I was hoping you'd get to see her. She was so excited to be going to a loving home that loved Jesus as much as she does. That's all she talks about. It's sweet, honestly."

Jacki nodded. "Our new patient, Ana. Can I leave a note with you for her charge nurse?"

"Yeah, hold on." Hannah fetched a pad of paper and Jacki wrote some notes as far as her thoughts on it being PMDD and to get an OB/GYN Consult, and possibly some hormone therapy. Hannah recognized the new name on the board. "That's not Ana from the ED, is it? What happened?" Jacki nodded and quickly explained the events of earlier this morning and headed for her next assignment. While waiting for the elevator, she checked her phone and saw she had a message from Kathryn.

Kathryn: Hey, working girl, would you like to meet for dinner tonight? I have something I want to talk to you about. And no, it's not bad.

Jacki: Sure! I'm not sure what time I'll be finished, it depends on if the ED has any interruptions for me. I'm aiming for 7, is that too late?

Kathryn: No, that's not too late for me. There are always light options, or just drinks. After the morning you've had, and still have the rest of the day, drinks might be the better option. Shoot me a text when you're close to leaving and we'll decide on a place.

Jacki: Sounds good. Talk to you then, off to SUD now. After I grab a snack, because I'm getting hungry.

Kathryn: Gee, can't imagine why, miss workaholic. Talk to you later. Hope the rest of your day is uneventful.

Jacki wondered what Kathryn wanted to talk about. She had heard rumors that she was considering retiring but had no idea what that would have to do with her. Shrugging her shoulders, she headed for the vending machines on the way to the SUD unit. Lauryn was in but the unit appeared a bit busy, so she just got to work on visiting her patients and making recommendations and referrals for those who were interested. More of their usual regulars, a few new faces who were first time addicts wanting to kick the habit. Jacki was thankful that she knew none of the patients on the floor, aside from the regulars. As she checked her last patient off, she glanced at the clock. 2:00. She had a few consultations on the Palliative Care unit left before her difficult case on the L&D floor. If she timed it correctly, she could be finished earlier than 7. As if someone read her thoughts, her ED pager went off:

Sexual Assault/rape. 15-year-old female. Wants to speak with a female chaplain.

Ugh. These are never good, Jacki thought to herself as she pivoted and headed for the stairwell down to the ED. She headed straight for Sara. "We meet again, my friend" Jacki said, as she reached for the young patient's chart. "Hello---hopefully this one will not start more trouble for you like this morning. Room 2 has Mary Jane Beckmeyer. 15, said she was sexually assaulted but didn't want to go into detail with any of us. We even tried getting a female doctor, but she's afraid someone will overhear her."

"Any idea what's going on? You have pretty good intuition."

"My gut instinct is its family related. We asked if we could call her parents and she got agitated and scared." Shit. Jacki thought to herself. This day just gets better and better. Jacki held her breath for a moment as she prepared to enter the room. She knocked faintly on the door, not to scare her. "Mary Jane? I'm Jacki, the chaplain."

Mary Jane looked up anxiously as Jacki closed the door tightly behind her. "These doors are 100% soundproof, Mary Jane. I promise nobody will hear anything. Sara, your nurse, told me you were sexually assaulted but wouldn't give them much information." Mary Jane nodded slowly. "I'm just so scared that someone out there would have heard me. I didn't realize the doors shut that tight." Jacki smiled. "Well, they do! So, what happened? What's going on, Mary Jane? Is someone at home hurting you?"

"Well---kind of. It's not at home, exactly. But my parents travel a lot for work, and I have to stay at my aunt and uncle's house for long periods of time. It's there that it happened."

Jacki could see where this was going but didn't want to assume or lose Mary Jane's trust. "What happened, Mary Jane? Did he touch you?" She nodded. "It's been happening for a while. It started out just simple things. He'd tickle me, or always seemed to enjoy me being around him. Had me sit on his lap, stuff like that. Whenever I'd tell my aunt, she'd just tell me that's how he is. Not to read into it." Jacki nodded silently. She knew how that felt, too. She encouraged her to continue. "Then, the past few weeks, it's been getting weirder. He wanted me to sit on his lap a certain way and had me bounce up and down. I did it once, but it made me uncomfortable, so I told him no. He tried that with me today and when I said no, he threw me on the bed and…." Mary Jane's voice cracked before she trailed off. Jacki took her hand. "It's okay. You did great, Mary Jane. I don't need to hear anymore. I know this is scary. And I'm so sorry this happened to you. But you're a minor. We need to notify the authorities about this. And your parents." Mary Jane hesitated at first. "Can you be with me when I tell them? When I talk to them? My parents are very strict and may not believe me at first."

"Of course, I will, Mary Jane. I'm here to help you through whatever it is you need, and if being beside you when you tell your parents and the police is what you need, I will do that. I can call them right here with you if you want. Nobody else needs to know. Chaplains have patient confidentiality except when the patient is in danger of harming themselves." Mary Jane agreed, and they made the phone call to her parents, who joined them at the hospital. They moved to the more private family room, which also had sound-proof doors. "Hello, I am Martin, and this is my wife, Joanne. Thank you for being with our daughter. It sounded like she had something important to share with us." Jacki glanced at Mary Jane before clearing her throat.

"Yes, I'm sorry to say your daughter has had something tragic happen to her this morning. It has been going on for a while, but she's been afraid to tell you about it. I encouraged her to share with you and promised her I would be here when she told you." Martin appeared to be listening intently, but Jacki noticed Joanne was already getting emotional. Martin caught Jacki's glance and realized Joanne's reaction. He appeared slightly concerned but turned his attention back to Mary Jane. "What is it, honey? You can tell us anything. I know we're not home a lot, but we love you very much and if something bad is happening at school, we need to know." Mary Jane glanced at Jacki and took a breath before beginning her saga. "It's not at school, daddy. It's at Uncle Louie's. He's been touching me. It started with small things and kept growing. He'd have me sit on his lap and rock back and forth or hop up and down. He'd make noises when I did that. Once I realized what he was doing, I stopped and said I wouldn't do that anymore. He tried to get me to do that this morning, but I told him no, and he pushed me on the bed and raped me." Jacki patted Mary Jane on the hand, in support of her being able to share her story. A couple female police officers had slid into the room just in time to hear the story as well. Mary Jane noticed them when she looked up. At first, she was scared, but quickly smiled and sighed a sigh of relief. She had begun the journey. She shared her story. Martin became very angry. Joanne had begun losing composure a few minutes into her daughter's story. "Oh, Mary Jane, I'm so sorry! I should have seen the signs. There were concerns with some of our other niece's, too, but I never thought they were true." Joanne turned to the police officers, and started giving any information they asked for, not concerned at all about hiding her brother's perverted actions any longer. The police officers and Mary Jane's parents stepped out into the hallway to begin the next steps of the investigation, leaving Mary Jane and Jacki alone. "You did so good, Mary Jane. I'm so proud of you. That took a lot of courage and bravery."

"Thanks, Jacki. I don't think I could have done it if it wasn't for you being with me. What's going to happen next? Am I going to get in trouble?" Jacki shook her head. "No, Mary Jane. I don't think you'll be in any trouble at all. Your parents may appear upset with you for not telling them sooner, but they just love you very much and want you to know you can trust them. They'll talk to the police, and the police will go and arrest your uncle. There will likely be court proceedings, and hopefully, if he is found guilty, he will be put away for a very long time." Mary Jane lowered her head for a few minutes. "I hope none of my cousins hate me. I don't want to lose my cousins."

Jacki inhaled sharply, not wanting to sound too blunt. "Honey, this is serious…what happened to you is serious. If your cousins choose not to believe you or choose to not talk to you because you went to an adult with his inappropriate behavior…then, they're not good cousins after all. Cousins are like your first best friends, and best friends stick by you no matter what. Do you understand?" Mary Jane nodded as a tear slipped down her cheek. "You did great, Mary Jane. I'm proud of you. I'm going to leave my card with you---please reach out to me if you need to talk. I've been in your shoes. I know everything you're feeling. I'm here for you. And your parents, too." Mary Jane asked for one last request before Jacki left---a hug. That meant progress to Jacki, as some people who go through sexual assault, especially with family members, want nothing to do with gestures of affection. They shared a hug and Jacki went out to speak briefly to her parents, giving them her card, also, and headed up to the Palliative Care unit.

This was only her first or second time on this unit since becoming a chaplain. She always loved the peaceful feeling the unit brought to visitors. The soft music piped into the ceiling, the beautiful stained-glass windows. Rosa was the unit secretary this afternoon. "Hi, Rosa!" Rosa turned at the sound of her name. "Jacki! How lovely to see you! We are not graced with your presence nearly enough on this unit. I must talk with Kathryn about that." Jacki laughed. "I'm meeting her for dinner tonight, I'll be sure to mention it. What do you have for me today?" Rosa shuffled through the papers on her desk to find the folder with chaplain/spiritual care consultations. "There we go---let's see, you have three today. Gary is in his 60s and has end stage renal failure. Stacia is the youngin' of the floor---She's only 35, Ovarian cancer. Sweet girl. And then there's Wilma. She's a ripe old 96 and ready to go. She's waiting for a bed at a hospice facility, but we don't think she'll make it to one." Jacki smiled. "Getting cases from you is always entertaining, Rosa. You make it interesting." "Hey, now what's that supposed to mean, young lady?" Jacki laughed. "Just as I said, your little animated thoughts and sayings make getting report from you interesting. It's a lot better than the cut and dry basics I get from others." Rosa followed her with a Rosa side-eye. "Alright, I'll take that as a compliment, this time. But I'm watching you, missy," she said in a mock tone. "Oh, look at me, I'm so scared" Jacki teased back as she headed towards Wilma's room.

Wilma's visit was quick, as she was a long time Baptist and knew where she was headed. She just loved to talk with people and didn't get many visitors, so always agreed to have the spiritual care department visit. Gary's visit was also rather quick. Although he was still young, he has been sick since he was a teenager with one thing or another, plus a lifetime of diabetes. He knew and accepted that his death meant the end of his earthly suffering. That left Stacia. Another difficult visit, as Ovarian cancer cases always bothered Jacki. She took a breath and headed towards her door, knocking on it, expecting to be interrupting a family surrounding her. Instead, she found only Stacia.

"Hello, Stacia. I'm Jacki, the chaplain assigned to this floor today. How are you feeling?" Jacki could tell that she was nearing the end of this painful journey. Her skin had begun mottling. Her chart mentioned that this was a more recent development.

"Sick. Tired. I'm trying to hold off as long as possible without morphine, but I think I'm ready now. This is no way to live." Jacki nodded. "Yes, Ovarian Cancer is not a nice creature. Have you accepted your diagnosis?" Stacia nodded. "Yeah. I'm not happy about it, but I'm ready."

"How did you find out you had ovarian cancer? If you don't mind me asking."

Stacia didn't respond for a few minutes, and Jacki saw a tear slide down her cheek. "It's sad to say, but if it wasn't for my little angel, I would've never known. You see, I was pregnant. About eight weeks. Something just didn't feel right, I knew I shouldn't have felt that much pressure in my abdomen that early in the pregnancy. I ended up miscarrying, and after that they did testing and determined that the pressure, I was feeling was a tumor on my ovary. It was competing for space with the growing baby. If I wasn't pregnant, I probably wouldn't have found it until much later. I think that's why I'm so ready to go---I know I'll get to meet my angel baby." Stacia smiled and Jacki could tell she was at peace with what was coming. "How is your family handling the diagnosis? I was surprised to find only you in here." Stacia sighed. "I don't have any family. My parents died, my husband left me once I got diagnosed, saying when he said our vows, he didn't mean death by cancer. He's some religious nut, no offense." Jacki laughed. "None taken. I'm a chaplain and I would even call him a nut at that point. That's insane. I'm so sorry." Stacia tried to grab Jacki's hand but sitting up straight hurt too much. "Don't be sorry for me. Death is not an enemy when your loved ones are waiting---I have both my parents, my angel baby, even my sister is waiting for me. She had childhood cancer. She was my best friend. I can't wait to see her again." Jacki nodded. "I suppose death would be a welcome friend, in that instance. I can relate to parts of that scenario. Are you aware of the hospice options available to you?" Stacia nodded. "Yeah, I'm waiting to hear about a bed at the Hope on the Hill one, it sounded so beautiful. My nurse said if it gets too much for me to wait, they can start the process here. I wouldn't mind that; it is peaceful here." Jacki had to agree. "What's preventing you from agreeing to beginning the process here?" "My own stubbornness" Stacia snickered. "I keep telling myself, one more day, you can make one more day. A bed may open tomorrow. But I think I'm about done waiting. I want to go peacefully, not in pain." They talked for a few more moments and Jacki agreed to let the nurse know on her way out if Stacia wished that she was ready to start the medication. Stacia nodded and thanked Jacki as she left. Once Jacki was done filling in the nurse on Stacia's decision and finishing her notes for all her patients, she headed to her office for a few minutes before she headed to her final patient of the day---one that would more than likely deplete her of the last ounce of emotional energy she had.

Chapter 10

Well, I can't hide from this case forever, Jacki thought to herself as she got out of her chair and headed for the Labor & Delivery unit. As she walked into the unit, she was greeted by Trina's compassionate smile.

"I knew it was going to be you. I was hoping it would be someone else, though, for your sake."

"Yeah, me too, honestly. But I guess it's my turn to be tested in this area. Which room are they in?"

Trina pointed to the room on the far right of the hallway. "Just look for the purple butterfly on the door." Jacki nodded as she headed in that direction. The purple butterfly program was something Mount Mercy implemented just a few months ago, to signify that a baby had been lost and to be respectful of the family behind the door who was grieving. Jacki was part of adapting that program, and sadly had been on the other side of the door herself a few years back. She took a breath and knocked on the door. "Come in" she heard in unison.

"Hi, Bethany. I'm Jacki, the hospital chaplain. I'm so sorry for your loss," she said in an almost robotic tone. It wasn't until she looked up that she saw a sight that ripped her heart. A young girl, about 10, with a "big sister" shirt on, was holding her lifeless little sister. Jacki took in the sight before turning her attention to the parents.

"Nice to meet you, Jacki. And thank you. This is such a new experience for us. We got pregnant with Melody right away. After she turned two, we started trying again. Nothing was happening. We had a couple early pregnancy losses, and then this baby seemed to be staying with us. I hadn't felt her move in a few hours and that was unlike her, so I came in to get checked out. That's when they told us she had passed, probably sometime yesterday. They induced me and she was born at 8 o'clock last night."

"I know all too well the pain you're feeling. I was here myself a few years ago. Not full-term, but still very difficult. How are you holding up? I'm sure it is still a shock."

Bethany nodded. "The staff here has been so great. They treated her like any other birth, allowing her to go right on my chest when she was born. They asked if I wanted the lullaby played when she was born. They even let Melody be in the room, like we had planned. The purple butterfly program is amazing." Jacki nodded in agreement. "I understand you wanted the baby baptized?" For the first time, Brandon spoke up. "Yes, it's very important to us. I wasn't aware chaplains could do baptisms, though."

"We can in hospital settings if the family requests it. Especially if they are not from around here, or do not have a priest that is willing to come to the hospital. I'd be happy to do it for you." Brandon and Bethany glanced at each other and nodded their heads in unison. Brandon helped his wife up once the small font was wheeled in.

"What is her name" Jacki asked. Bethany looked at Melody. "We promised, baby. If it was a girl, you could pick her name." Melody looked back at her little sister, trying to determine what her name would be. "Mallory. Mallory Raelynn" she said with a smile.

"Wow, Melody! That's a beautiful name" Jacki said, looking into her eyes. "Especially the middle name. Can I have your baby sister for a moment? I promise I'll give her right back." Jacki noticed a small smile come over Bethany's face. "I baptize you Mallory Raelynn Lacroix, in the name of the father, son, and Holy Spirit. You are now a child of God." It was a quick ceremony, but meaningful to the grieving family. As promised, she dried Mallory off and handed her back to her big sister. She decided to take a little time to talk with Melody. "You love your little sister, don't you, Melody?" Melody nodded. "I just don't understand why she can't stay with me. With us. We've all waited so long for me to be a big sister. I guess I'm not supposed to be one."

"Melody, you are a big sister. I know it's not the same as taking her home, having her to play with and grow up together, but she is still very much your little sister. I can't predict what will happen in the future, perhaps Jesus will bless your mommy and daddy with another baby, but regardless, this little baby sister will always be yours. Jesus picked you to be her big sister. Do you know why?" Melody shook her head as tears started to form. "No, why?"

"Because he sees how much you loved her, from the moment you found out you were going to be her big sister. It takes a special person to be a big sister to a baby that gets returned to heaven. They must remember them, talk about them with others, and make them proud. Jesus saw something special in you, and knew you'd be the perfect person to be little Mallory's big sister. Just like he chose your mommy and daddy." Melody stared into Mallory's lifeless face with such love. It nearly knocked Jacki to the floor. Suddenly, Melody looked up. "Do you want to hold her, Jacki? I heard you talking to my mommy about your baby. Jesus chose you, too." Jacki couldn't breathe for a few moments, the impact of her words hit her so hard. She blinked back tears as she nodded. "I would love to, Melody." Jacki took little Mallory in her arms and held her for a few minutes. She tried to keep her composure, not wanting to fall apart in front of the family she was sent to minister to. "She really is beautiful, Bethany."

"Perfect in every way, just too perfect for this world." Bethany said quietly. "What you said to Melody was beautiful. Thank you. She's been so strong, but I know how much it hurts her. I feel like we're failing her. She'd be the best big sister. I guess she is, just in a different way than we imagined." Jacki asked Melody if she could put the baby back in her cradle, before turning to Bethany. "She is the best big sister to Mallory. I have no doubt that their bond will remain, despite Mallory not being able to come home with you. She is a very sensitive, smart little girl for her age. Never discourage her from talking about Mallory. Grieve as a family. Obviously, your grief will look slightly different, being that you carried her, but she is loved and missed equally by all of you." Jacki was about to leave when Melody came up to Jacki. "How old was your baby? Was it a girl or a boy baby?" Bethany held her breath and Brandon went to scold her for asking such a personal question, but Jacki stopped him mid-sentence. "Don't. It's okay, I just finished telling all of you to never hide your child, so I must swallow my own medicine." She turned to Melody. "I was 25 weeks. So, Mallory was a few months older than my baby when she was born. I named her Melanie. Melanie Faith. She was a lot tinier than your sister but losing her was just as difficult. After she was born, the doctors found out I couldn't have any more babies, so Melanie is my only baby." Melody looked away for a moment and then gave Jacki a big hug. "I know it must hurt. But maybe she knows Mallory now, and they're playing together. All babies go to the same place when they die, don't they?" Jacki was amazed at this young girl's words. "I believe so, yes. And that is a beautiful image. I hope you can think of that, too, when missing Mallory gets more difficult. She's not alone, she has a friend in heaven. And she's watching all of you." Jacki left her card with the family and encouraged them to call anytime, making it a point to include Melody as well. Once she cleared the hallway, she found the nearest bathroom and splashed cold water on her face to hide the red, puffy eyes. She glanced at her watch. It was 5:30. She walked to the clock and punched out and messaged Kathryn. They decided to go to their usual spot. Needing the walk for mental health reasons, Jacki opted to cross the street instead of taking the footbridge. Once she got outside, she quickly regretted that decision. I really need a parking spot where my remote starter can work, Jacki thought as she climbed into her car and let it warm up. It had been a very difficult day. It felt like she had worked a 24-hour shift, energy wise. She was looking forward to some down time talking with Kathryn. She walked and found Kathryn sitting in a corner.

"Why do we live in a state where we can't feel our faces?" Jacki said, as she slid into the booth.

"Because there are no earthquakes, spiders, snakes, or alligators?" Kathryn responded.

"True that!" Jacki agreed, as she ordered a drink from the bar.

"Rough day?" Kathryn teased, gesturing toward the bar. Jacki nodded. Sexual Assault case. Family member. Sometimes, I just don't understand how people can abuse their own family members like that. I know it's a disease of sorts, but, dang. I enjoyed my time on the Palliative Care unit though, I'm not there hardly enough."

"How's Stacia? Still holding on? That woman is stubborn as a mule."

"She finally agreed to start the end-of-life medications. She is a tough woman though. Wilma is just too stinking cute." Kathryn laughed. "Oh, Wilma. Dear woman's been around forever and is clearly ready to leave us, but we will all feel it when she goes." Kathryn let the silence hang for a few minutes. "How did it go with the stillborn?" Jacki didn't answer right away, but instead looked away. "I'm sorry, Jacki. I didn't think when I assigned you to that." "Stop" Jacki said. "It's not your fault. You could not have predicted the events of the day, the late miscarriage in the ED, what happened with Ana…it's not just that case that is affecting me today, it's all of them. But it's part of our job. And I must learn to accept my own sorrows while helping others. If anything, that stillborn case helped me peel another layer off."

Kathryn noticed the tone shift in Jacki's voice. "How so? What happened?"

"I had a moment with their daughter. The 10-year-old. It was quite special, honestly. She asked me about my own baby because she overheard me talking to her mom about losing a baby of my own. She asked me if I wanted to hold her." Kathryn sighed. "I knew there was something special about that kid. She's just made differently than others. I'm sure it's hard on her, she was so excited to be a big sister. Did you hold the baby?"

"I did. For a few minutes. She was so perfect. Just like Melanie was. They named her Mallory Raelynn. Well, Melody named her, I should say."

Their food arrived shortly after. After a few bites, Jacki broke the ice. "So, you said you had something you wanted to talk to me about?"

Kathryn swallowed and took a breath. "Well, you know how I've been talking about wanting to retire?"

"Yes, I've heard rumors that you decided to. Are you retiring, Kath? Is it true?"

"Well, yes. But exactly when, depends on what you're going to say to me next."

Jacki looked at her with a confused expression. "What do I have to do with your decision to retire? I mean, I'll obviously miss you like crazy, but I'd want you to be happy. If you feel it's time, then do it."

"I need a replacement, Jacki. I can't retire until someone agrees to take the Director of Spiritual Care position. I've talked with the hospital board, and despite you only being here a year and a half, they feel you have the drive and compassion that the program needs. I personally feel the Spiritual Care department would thrive under your young-blooded leadership. Even your fellow colleagues agree."

Jacki couldn't believe what she was hearing. She had just made ED chaplain status a few weeks ago, and now Kathryn wanted to make her Director of Spiritual Care!

"Kathryn---are you sure about this? You don't think anyone will say something, being that I was just promoted to ED chaplain?"

"So, what if they do, Jacki? It's just words. If they are not adult enough to be supportive and encouraging to a staff member who is advancing, then their opinion doesn't really matter to begin with. So, what do you say? I understand if you need time to think about it, especially with all you've faced the past few shifts."

"No, no. I don't need time. I will take it. I'm honored to take it. I have big shoes to fill, but I know I have the support of my staff, and my God will equip me with what I need to make sure Mount Mercy is known for their Spiritual Care Department."

Kathryn's smile beamed with excitement. "I'm so happy to hear that, Jacki. As soon as I started contemplating deeply about retirement, I knew I wanted you to replace me. I had that on the back burner when I promoted you. I will announce it tomorrow during morning meeting."

They enjoyed the rest of their meals and opted for dessert, to celebrate Jacki's big promotion. Over cheesecake, Kathryn broached the subject of Ana. "How is our environmental specialist, Ana? Did you get to visit her?"

Jacki put her fork down and wiped a crumb from her mouth. "I did. She seemed in great spirits. At first was afraid I'd give her the 'Jesus doesn't approve of suicide' talk, but once I calmed her nerves, she started to share. I put in for a hormonal and OB/GYN consult for her." Kathryn seemed surprised at first, but then understood. "You're thinking PMDD?" Jacki was surprised. "You know what that means?!" Kathryn nodded. "My sister had it. We all thought she was headed for a sparkly straight jacket and basket weaving, but her GYN did labs and found her hormone levels to be way out of whack. Diagnosed her and got her on some hormone meds and she's a completely different woman. She passed a few years ago of a heart attack, but she was the Peggy I remember in the end, not the nutzo she was before."

Jacki laughed. "You come up with the funniest words, Kath. I think I'm going to miss those more than anything."

"Hey!" Kathryn shouted. "I'm retiring, I'm not dead. You'll still hear from me, and I will be sure to visit. Even though I'm announcing it tomorrow, I don't plan to officially step down until after the Mount Mercy awards night in June. Which, speaking of, you're going to, right?" Jacki eyed her with suspicion. "I don't usually participate in those type of events, but since I'm becoming a Department Director, I suppose I have to get used to them, don't I?" Kathryn smiled. "Yes, I suppose you would. Besides, it's fun to get dressed up fancy and support and celebrate your fellow colleagues. You can even invite as many friends as you want." Jacki sighed. "I guess I better get back into those weight loss shakes and find a dress, then, huh?" Kathryn didn't answer but had a suspicious grin on her face. "You don't have anything else up your sleeve, do you?" "I plead the fifth." Kathryn said, throwing her hands up in surrender. "Seriously, though, department heads are not allowed to talk about the awards banquet other than in general." Jacki nodded slowly, giving her the investigator side-eye she was known for. "Well, this was a wonderful night, Kathryn. I needed to just relax and chat. And thank you, again, for recommending me to take your position. As nervous as I am, I'm also excited for the future. My future, as well as the future of Mount Mercy's Spiritual Care Department." They shared a hug and agreed they would see each other tomorrow at the morning meeting for the big announcement. Once inside her car, Jacki called Alisha right away on the speaker phone.

"Hey, Jacki. What's up? Everything okay? You never call me."

Jacki laughed. "Yeah, well, special events call for special services. Want to hear something cool?"

"Did you adopt Susie? Did something happen with her going to Donna's family? You sound so happy."

"No, she left with them this morning. It's even better than that, honestly. Are you at Sandie's? I'll be driving right by there on my way home, I can just stop over."

"Yeah, my house is getting worked on, so I'm back at Sandie's for a little bit. She's out at her Women's group, but she should be home shortly. Do we need wine glasses?"

Jacki thought for a moment. She had already had one drink at the restaurant, but she always had a change of clothes in her car for emergencies, she could just sleep over Sandie's and leave early to walk her dog before heading to work.

"Take out the Mud Slide glasses. It's a celebratory night. I always have clothes in the car, I'll just spend the night."

Jacki pulled in right behind Sandie. "Jacki! I'm so surprised to see you, is everything alright?" Jacki smiled. "Great, actually. I called Alisha a while ago and wanted to come over to share some exciting news with you guys. There will be celebratory drinks involved, so I'm spending the night here, if that's alright with you."

"Absolutely!" Sandie exclaimed. "I love unexpected women sleepovers." They walked in together; Alisha was waiting in the kitchen for them. "OK, now that you're both here, can you please tell me what's going on? I'm dying over here!" Sandie chimed in. "Would you let me put my coat away first? And maybe we should sit down?" Jacki laughed. "Yes, how about we go sit in the living room and talk first, and then we can get the sleepover shenanigans started."

They sat down in the living room as Jacki began with small details about her exhausting day. She was good at building excitement and knew that they both enjoyed hearing about the patients she sees throughout the day. Sandie, especially, would always try to ask for updates on prior patients. "One of our hospital cleaners, Ana, was on the roof this morning, she was planning to jump. Ironically, I was on the nursery floor when I heard the noises from the roof appear louder than normal, and noticed the door was open. I went up to see what was going on and somehow managed to deescalate her and get her away from the edge." Sandie looked at her with amazement. "Wow, Jacki. Thank goodness you were observant. Jumping from a hospital rooftop would have caused a lot more damage than to just Ana. How is she doing?" "She's doing better. I saw her this afternoon once she got admitted to the unit. We had the usual chat I have with all suicides and overdoses. I honestly think hers was caused by PMDD." Alisha sat up straight. "I've heard of that! That's when your hormones go way out of whack, right?" Jacki nodded. "Yes. It can sometimes cause people to become suicidal, but also homicidal. It's more common with PMS aged women but can at times happen during the onset of menopause, which I believe is what happened with Ana."

"What were you doing at the nursery," Sandie asked. "With what you went through, that's the last place I'd expect you to be." Jacki sighed. "Well, after I left the miscarriage case with the hot-headed doctor that I was able to get removed from the hospital roster, I needed to cool down. Plus, the emotions of the miscarriage itself brought back memories. When I need to go sit with that memory, the nursery window is where I go. Now, though, I'm thinking God sent me there so I would be able to deescalate Ana." Alisha nodded. "Could be. I know people who have a strong spiritual life can sometimes sense things like that, or suddenly find themselves going someplace they weren't planning on, only to find someone in need there."

Jacki continued sharing about her time on the Palliative Care Unit, as well as the stillborn. Jacki couldn't help tearing up as she shared with Alisha and Sandie how touching little Melody was, holding her sister and then having a moment with Jacki. By the time she shared what Melody had said, she was struggling to remain in control of her emotions. Sandie reached over and patted her hand. "It's okay. Your tears are safe here with us. I know your pain all too well, as you know. Don't hide them, Jacki." Jacki allowed herself to let go of the emotions of both the little innocent babies she baptized today, the emotions that brought up, and her own memories that haunted her regarding Melanie's loss. Sandie simply held her in that moment until she was able to be okay again. She wiped her eyes and sniffled. "Thanks, Sandie. Sometimes you just need that other person to look at you and say 'hey, let go. I'm here.' That's the hardest thing about Melanie, is I have nobody. Others say they understand, but when I go to talk about it, or when I have experiences at work that bring it back, they want nothing to do with it. So, I just do what I can to comfort myself, but it doesn't always work." Sandie nodded. "Oh, yes. The 'I'm here for you, but only if it fits my time schedule' I know those people well. But you can always lean on me. I'll gladly be that person for you. I believe in her. I may have been a few weeks ahead of you when I lost Jacob, but that does not make your loss any less real than mine. You have a right to feel your emotions and triggers without being judged or criticized. I can promise you that will never happen here. This can be your safe space for Melanie." Jacki hugged Sandie. "I've been praying to God a lot lately. Asking him to send me someone that I can go to with Melanie. I understand it makes some people uncomfortable, others just don't have the compassion to listen and be present. Others don't even know because I'm so good at keeping it to myself. But I told Melody that she had the responsibility of being Mallory's big sister even if she's not physically here, so I guess I need to do the same with Melanie. I just didn't think I'd be able to find someone I could share with, without getting the usual responses."

"Well, I'm right here, dear Jacki. You've found someone that will listen and understand exactly what you're feeling. We'll remember Melanie just as we remember Jacob." Jacki took a breath and composed herself. "Now that all the depressing things are out of the way, I can talk about the part we're celebrating." Both Sandie and Alisha made it a point to look at her finger. "Still no ring, so it's not that." Jacki laughed. "Again, that requires a boyfriend. Not happening."

"Well, you just got promoted, so it can't be that again" Alisha said. After a few minutes watching Jacki's facial expression, Sandie asked "can it?" Jacki nodded slowly, with an excited smile on her face.

"Kathryn's retiring at the end of June and offered me the Director of Spiritual Care position." Alisha squealed and Sandie jumped excitedly. "Oh, Jacki that's wonderful! I am so proud of you, and I'm sure your dad and Melanie are just as excited and proud. You've accomplished so much in the last few years, putting yourself through school with little support, losing Melanie. You made a name for yourself despite your circumstances, and it is so inspiring." Jacki was tearing up all over again. She still struggled heavily with praise and compliments. "Thanks, Sandie. It's not easy for the average person, but when you have a broken mind from abuse, it is even more of a challenge. I hope my dad is proud of me. I think of him, especially when I get the SUD assignment. Sometimes I even feel like he's walking beside me. Same with Melanie when I have babies like Mallory and Serenity. I did it for them more than me, I think, sometimes."

"They are proud of you, Jacki" Alisha chimed in. "And so am I. You probably don't know this, but during chaplaincy school there were times where I questioned if I was headed in the right direction, and you always encouraged me. Reminded me that my gifts are in this field and I belong here." Jacki was surprised. "I had no idea you were struggling so much, Alisha. I'm glad I could help you find your way, and you are an amazing hospice chaplain. We may be in different environments, but our calling and mission is still the same."

They opened another round of mudslides and celebrated Jacki's new title. Jacki shared with them the date of the awards banquet and said she needed to go dress shopping and needed them both for fashion advice. "You know me, broken mind, always think I look ugly in every dress I try on. If I went myself, I'd arrive to the banquet in jeans and a dress shirt."

"Well, that will not be happening on my watch!" Sandie exclaimed. "I happen to love dress shopping. There are so many stores, if we start looking now, we might be able to find a good one, before prom season hits." They stayed up a while longer, talking about whatever came to mind, before turning in for the night. Jacki had to be at the morning meeting tomorrow morning, but otherwise had the day off. She decided she was going to go on a special drive to someplace she had not been in a long time. Someplace she needed to visit. She thought of asking Sandie to go with her, but decided it was something she must do alone.

Chapter 11

Jacki woke up at her usual 6:00, showered and was planning on making breakfast, but by the time she got out of the shower, Sandie had already beaten her to the kitchen. She also found a paper bag lunch with a smiley face on a post-it note waiting for her. *I don't know about that woman* she thought to herself. She had coffee with Sandie, and they did morning prayer together. "Where's Alisha?" Jacki asked. Sandie took a sip of her coffee just as Jacki asked the question. "She got called in the middle of the night for a hospice patient. You never realize that chaplains get those late-night calls, too, until you live with one." Jacki nodded. It was a rarity, but Jacki also at times would get woken in the middle of the night, especially with being the ED chaplain. If a trauma came in that needed a Spiritual Care provider, Jacki was the lucky winner. "She is so good at what she does, though." Jacki said, sipping her coffee. "Hopefully she'll get home and get some sleep. What's on your agenda today, Sandie?"

Sandie thought for a moment. "Nothing really. I might do some work in the garden since the sun is shining today. Other than that, probably my usual baking, or reading. What about you?"

Jacki thought for a moment about how to answer that question. "Well, I have a morning meeting with the Spiritual Care team. I think Kathryn's planning to announce her retirement and that I am taking her place, which I'm sure will ruffle a few feathers. But, otherwise, I'm off today. I plan to take a drive in the sunshine and go someplace I haven't been to in a long while. The events of the past few days warrant a trip." Jacki trailed off, not wanting to think any further. Sandie was always good at picking up body language cues and knew right away what that trip meant.

"Going to visit someone special, are we?" Sandie said with a smile. Jacki nodded. She was afraid to say anything more out loud, for fear of her emotions cracking. Sandie touched her hand. "Do you want me to go with you?" Jacki thought for a moment, and almost agreed, but declined. "No but thank you. I need to go by myself this time." Sandie nodded. "I understand. I remember those days with Jacob. For months, I would avoid that place like the plague. But when I'd finally visit, I'd get it all out and feel better. Just know I'm here for you, you can call me if you change your mind, or if you're struggling harder than expected and need me to meet with you."

"Thanks, Sandie. It means a lot. I probably will stop by again on my way home, to cry on someone's shoulder, but I just feel I need to do this by myself. To just sit with them both and talk into the air."

Sandie took Jacki's empty coffee cup to the sink and hugged her tightly. "I know exactly what you mean. I'll be here. Have a good meeting and a safe trip." Jacki thanked Sandie for breakfast and headed out the door.

The ride to the hospital was uneventful, which was surprising considering it was a school day. She pulled in and found a parking space close to the entrance. Morning meetings always included coffee and donuts, so Jacki would save some money not needing to buy coffee inside. She took the elevator to the top floor, where the Spiritual Care office was. Once everyone was in attendance, Kathryn began the meeting with a prayer, handed out assignment folders to those who were on today's schedule and began the rest of the meeting.

"Before we break down our daily assignments, I have an announcement to make. Many of you know that my husband has been ill. While he is much better now, I have made the difficult decision to step down and retire from this position, to spend the remaining time with him. I have held this job for many years and this decision was not taken lightly. I am not stepping down until the end of June, after the Mount Mercy awards banquet. I am pleased to announce that Jacki Redmond is taking my position, effective July 1st. Jacki, although new to the hospital staff, is an amazing asset to our team and I feel has the dedication, compassion, and drive to make Mount Mercy's Spiritual Care Unit thrive. I understand that her age and years of experience may anger some of you, but I ask that you treat her with respect and come together as a team to share the common mission of Mount Mercy Spiritual Care."

Much to Jacki's surprise, everyone clapped for her and genuinely seemed happy for her. She thanked everyone for their support, and Kathryn for recommending her for such a highly esteemed and valued position on the team. After the morning meeting, a few of the chaplains came up to congratulate Jacki. They chatted for a few minutes, before heading for their assigned units. Kathryn waited until everyone had left, before approaching Jacki. "Bet it felt weird not getting an assignment binder today."

Jacki laughed. "A little. For a split second, I was like 'hey, you forgot somebody', but I'm glad I have the day off." Kathryn nodded. "Yeah, these past few shifts have been rather eventful for you, haven't they?" "You could say that. Just brought up a lot of personal stuff for me too. The babies, getting offered your position." Kathryn looked at Jacki with concern. "You're not having second thoughts, are you?" "Oh, goodness, no! I just mean what you said to me that day when we were out for dinner. How proud you are of me...just made me think of my dad." Kathryn nodded. "Ah. Having a memory stroll moment. I get it. So, what are you going to do with your day off? It's supposed to be nice today."

"It is." Jacki said. "Perfect day for a drive. I'm going someplace I haven't been in a long time. It's needed, after these last few days. After that, probably go to Sandie's and chill, or maybe go for a run."

"Sounds like a perfect day to me, minus the trip, as that sounds painful. I wish you a blessed day, Jacki. You're an amazing asset to our team and I'm looking forward to hearing amazing things about Mount Mercy in my retirement." Jacki thanked Kathryn and gave her a hug and headed out the door. It felt weird leaving the hospital, but it was a much-needed day off.

Jacki went home and walked her dog and changed into a pair of comfortable pants and her Mount Mercy Sweatshirt. Her dog sensed that she was having an emotional moment and kept trying to head-butt her the entire walk. "I'm okay, girl" Jacki told her dog, giving her a pat on the head. She let the dog back inside and then grabbed the lunch Sandie had made and headed back to the car. She played her favorite Christian music station for the drive, to clear her head and prepare her heart for the emotional visit that would happen.

As Jacki turned into Mount Mercy cemetery, she was greeted by an active funeral service blocking the gate she normally used. Luckily, she came here often for running, and knew alternate routes to get where she needed to be. Jacki loved these large garden style cemeteries. They were so filled with nature and beautiful statuary. Pulling up to the large statue she always parked near, she took a breath, grabbed her water bottle and lunch, and got out of the car. There was nobody in the area, which made Jacki happy. She laid a blanket down and sat staring at the stone shaped like an angel wrapped around a heart. Although grief is tricky, nothing triggers the memories much like seeing the name of a loved one written on a stone: Anthony Redmond 1955-2005. It had been a while since Jacki made the trip to visit her father's grave. Her sister Amy visited often, but Jacki never dared to make the trip unless she had to. The last time she was here was probably when she laid to rest the other name on the stone: Melanie Rose Redmond Born into heaven April 16, 2015.

Jacki took a breath and stared at both names. Her father had died young, after a lifelong battle of diabetes and heart issues. Her precious daughter was born stillborn, and doctors had no idea why. Both losses were huge blows for Jacki. She sat and reflected, letting the tears and other emotions surface.

Her counselor had told her sometimes all that's needed is to speak to them as if they're in front of you. That is what prompted this visit, along with the many events of her last few shifts. She waited a few minutes before just beginning to talk, letting the emotions out:

Daddy---I know it's been a while since I visited you. I wish you were here. You'd be so proud of me. Losing you shook me deeper than I thought it ever could. But I got back up. I did something with my life, something you and I both knew meant a lot to me. I'm a chaplain now, at a hospital. I even got a promotion to Director of Spiritual Care! I love my job, daddy, but it's so hard sometimes. I see cases that remind me of you, of what an amazing bond we shared. I was so mad at you, you know---for leaving me so young. I wouldn't want you suffering like you were, but you still left me. Seeing Maggie go through those emotions with her dad brought them all back for me. Please, don't be mad at me for not visiting. I'm going to try to visit more often.

She stopped a moment and let the emotions surface, as if she was waiting for a response from someone who wasn't there. She knew he wasn't there, nor was her daughter. Her faith taught her that their souls are in heaven. But she found such comfort in coming here today. Just to talk to her dad, and her daughter:

Melanie---mommy misses you so much. There are so many questions that will never be answered. Why God needed you, why he chose me to be strong enough to be a mother to a child that wasn't even here. I don't feel strong some days, baby girl. I wish more than anything that you were here. People say I may not be where I am today if I had you. But I don't believe that. I believe I would have found a way. Mommy has a great job that she loves. But sometimes that job reminds me so much of you, and the pain of losing my little girl. You were so perfect in every way. I'll always cherish those few short moments of holding you. Holding Mallory, the other day made me think of you. But Melanie, mommy really misses you. It's hard carrying your memory alone. I have nobody who understands. They said they did when it first happened. But now that it's been a few years, they expect me to just be done with it. Mommy tries to heal, she's still healing. But nobody listens anymore. I have Sandie to talk to, she's been in this place, too. But it's been so hard carrying your memory by myself. I hope I make you proud, baby girl.

Everything I do, I think of you. I know you wouldn't want your mommy to be sad all the time. You'd want me to use my pain to help others. Please watch over mommy. It hurts a lot lately, lots of reminders of you and what I went through. I love you so much. I wanted nothing more in life than to be your mommy. I can't be a mommy to other babies, you're all I have. It hurts so much. Please keep praying for mommy. Mommy loves you.

Jacki continued staring at the stone until it became blurry from a flood of tears forming. At first, she fought them back, but quickly decided to just let them go. This was why she was here. To feel her emotions. To let them be free. She has held them in for so long, always telling others it's okay to cry, to feel what is there--- but never listening to her own advice. Today was about her. Today was about freedom and allowing herself the same mercy and forgiveness. She broke down completely. She did not care if anyone was around her, she just let all the emotions come pouring out. Suddenly, as Jacki was crying, the sun suddenly became brighter and seemed to be shining directly on her. She looked up and felt a gentle breeze and all the pain and guilt she'd been hiding suddenly felt...gone. She felt relief and even her breathing felt lighter. She dried her eyes and walked back to the car, heading for Sandie's house.

Sandie welcomed her with open arms when Jacki pulled into the driveway. "I've been thinking of you all day. How did it go?" Jacki hugged her and sighed. "It was rough in spots; I'm not going to lie. I had no idea how much I was holding inside, until it started to tumble out. But the weirdest thing happened---I was recovering from my total breakdown when the sun suddenly got brighter, and a gentle breeze rolled by. It was so special." Sandie smiled. "Our loved ones do that sometimes, especially when they know we need it. That was probably your dad and Melanie letting you know they heard your words. They always do." Jacki followed Sandie inside the house. As usual, Sandie had been baking and the house smelled amazing. Jacki saw a plate on the table. "Those are not those mozzarella stuffed croissants you make, are they?"

Sandie smiled. "Yep. I figured what better comfort food for an emotional visit, than cheese?" Sandie poured some lemonade for them and served up a few of the croissants. Once they were on the deck, Sandie asked Jacki more about her special visit. "You said you didn't know how much you were holding in, what did you mean?"

"I don't know how to explain it" Jacki began, "Not so much with my dad, because it's been a while. He was more just emotions over wishing he were here to see all I've done. But

Melanie, I was carrying a lot of grief, and some guilt. Wondering why I couldn't have her, processing the fact that she's all I'll have. Missing her so much, with all the cases I've had this week that reminded me of losing her." Sandie put her arms around Jacki and looked her in the eye. "Why didn't you talk to me, Jacki? You knew I've been in those shoes. It's not your fault. I know they never determined what caused her death, but it most certainly was not you. I know it's hard to believe that--- we as mothers want to know why, even if we point blame on ourselves."

"I didn't know you very well" Jacki said, shrugging her shoulders. "So many others that I've tried to share with ended up walking away, or saying I needed help because I should be over it by now. I guess I just decided to keep it inside, instead of trying to look for someone. I started praying that God would send me a friend that I could share with, and he sent me you now. I know it happens in his time, just like healing happens when it's meant to, and not when others say so." Sandie nodded in agreement. "I remember those days. My Jacob was a full-term loss, we had a funeral and everything, and people still would tell me to just have another baby. That I had to think of my other children, and not grieve his loss. Alisha became that person for me, as crazy as it sounds." Jacki smiled, as she wiped a stray tear away. "Yeah, she told me that story. And now I have you. I'd love to listen to your story someday, and I'll share mine." Sandie said she'd like that, and they agreed to make time for each other. They talked for a few minutes before Jacki got up. "Well, as I'm sure you know, crying makes you quite tired. I'm going to head home and take a nap. Veronica and Marc are graduating tomorrow morning, and I don't want to look like a zombie at their graduation." Sandie walked her out to her car and gave her a long hug. Jacki drove off and headed home to her dog and her comfortable bed. It had been a long morning, but one that was necessary and very healing for Jacki. For the first time in a while, Jacki felt the freedom of forgiveness. She forgave herself for the loss of her daughter. She allowed herself to feel her grief for the first time since the loss. And she now had a friend who would listen to those emotions. Something she had wanted for years.

Chapter 12

Jacki spent the remainder of her day off with her dog and ordered from her favorite restaurant for dinner. A day of emotional healing required comfort food, a soak in the hot tub and a drink. She turned in early and awoke early the next morning.

While this day would not be as emotional for Jacki, it still had a lot going on. First up was a happy event, Veronica, and Marc's SAP Graduation ceremony. The ceremony was held at the treatment center. The drive was lovely for this time of year. Jacki felt an early spring on the horizon. She chose her black skirt and a sapphire blue shirt. Once she arrived at the facility, she immediately went to find a seat. She wanted to be up front so she could get good pictures. Veronica and Marc looked so happy in their new lives. Veronica was given her teaching job back, and they found a place for her to live where she would have a few other sisters in the same house. Marc, although he was graduating from the program, was granted permission to continue living on the premises until he was able to find his own housing. Instead of being taken off the police force entirely, his boss made him a DARE officer for the Puppington school district. After the ceremony, there was a small gathering for graduates and their friends and family. Jacki went and found Veronica and Marc, and had pictures taken with them. She was getting ready to leave when Marc spoke.

"Jacki, before you go, Veronica and I have a card for you. It's not much, but neither one of us would have the life we have today, the sobriety and freedom from drug use if it wasn't for you. Veronica can go back to being a teacher, and I can still say I'm a police officer, even if it's not on the city streets. We promise we will continue to stay on this path." Jacki blushed. "You guys didn't have to get me anything. Just like you have your jobs, this is part of mine. I am glad that I was able to minister to you and get you into a treatment program that worked. I will keep in contact with both of you. I am so proud of you both." They shared a group hug, before Jacki left and headed to the second event of her busy day---this one was sure to not be as happy, and the outcome was unknown.

Jacki pulled into the Puppington County Court Complex and found a parking spot---the last visitor's spot. Hopefully that's a good omen, Jacki thought to herself. She walked in and put her bag on the belt as she walked through security. The security guard asked her which case she was here for and led her to the correct court room. Mary Jane was already inside. She found a seat behind her and tapped her on the shoulder. "Jacki!" Mary Jane exclaimed. "I'm so glad you came for me." Her parents also displayed their gratitude. "I know this probably isn't the best part of your job, having to testify in court." Jacki shrugged. "You take the good with the bad, it's been a while since I had to testify. I have another case at the end of March I'm attending, but not testifying for."

Jacki turned off her phone and waited for the court hearing to begin. Two of Mary Jane's cousins also came forward, after hearing of her experience, which made this case more serious. Out of the corner of her eye, she saw a news reporter, but it was not her sister.

Once the proceedings started, Jacki was called up to the witness stand and sworn in.

"Welcome, Jacki. I understand you work as a chaplain for Mount Mercy Medical Center?"

"I do. The Emergency Department is my primary assignment."

"You were assigned to the department the afternoon of Mary Jane's attack, correct?"

"I was."

"And did you feel, upon first meeting Mary Jane, that her claims were trustworthy, given her age?"

"I did. She appeared very anxious, and would not speak in detail to anyone else, including medical personnel. This is common with sexual assault victims."

"So, why then, did she trust you?" Mary Jane's attorney yelled "Objection," to which the judge replied that she did not feel that question needed to be answered, sustaining the objection from defense. The prosecuting attorney continued to ask questions that Jacki felt did not pertain to the case. The final straw was bent when the prosecutor asked if she felt Mary Jane was competent.

"I absolutely feel that Mary Jane is a competent teenager. Regardless of why her parents still feel the need for her to stay with someone while they are away on business, Mary Jane is capable of handling herself. You are a prosecutor; you should know the laws better than anyone else. There is a law in this state that says any minor still attending school must be in the presence of an adult when they will be left alone for more than a few days at a time. Regardless of how you feel about this law, Mary Jane did not deserve to be sexually assaulted. That, your honor, is the issue here. The lifestyle choices her parents make for her have nothing to do with what happened to poor Mary Jane, and her two cousins who have also come forward. The scientific testing proves that she was, indeed, sexually assaulted. The DNA matches the defendant's uncle, as does the DNA of both cousins, from what has already been presented in this trial. If this man is not taken off the streets, there will only be more Mary Jane's. He seems to be attacking family members, but if one is capable of sexually assaulting one's own family members, there is no self-control and no stopping them from preying on other innocent victims."

A silence fell over the courtroom that Jacki had never experienced before. The prosecutor took a breath and said, "no further questions, your honor." Shortly after that, the jury left for deliberation, leaving Mary Jane, her family, and Jacki in the courtroom. In record setting time, just a mere two hours later, they had a verdict. GUILTY! Mary Jane's uncle was found guilty of THREE counts of sexual assault of a minor. He would be locked away for many years, never able to touch another innocent child again. After the announcement, her uncle was escorted out by the court guards. Mary Jane's father met his brother-in-law's gaze with anger and betrayal. As he was walking by, Mary Jane's father stopped the guards so he could speak to his brother-in-law. "I hope you rot in that jail cell. How dare you betray our family. Not only did you touch Mary Jane, but we also find out you touched other family members. Young, innocent family members. You are one sick man." He looked at the guards and told them to carry him out. He then turned to his daughter and gave her a tearful hug. "I'm so proud of you, baby. I know how hard that was to tell the judges what happened. You did so good." "Thank you, daddy." Mary Jane said. "It's because Jacki was there. When I got scared, or talking about it made me remember it more, I just looked at her and it calmed me down." She turned to Jacki and gave her a hug. "You have done so much for our daughter." Her mother said. "The fact that you would give of your time to be here and testify on her behalf shows that you truly care about those you serve. How could we ever thank you?" Jacki shook her head in reply. "There is no need to thank me. It is my job. I do anything for the people I meet in their darkest hours, even if it stretches far into the future. I care about every single one of my assigned patients. They are more than just a name on a checklist to me, they are real people who need support." They talked for a few more minutes, until the news reporter began approaching the family. "And the oncoming news anchor is my cue to leave" Jacki said with a laugh. "I don't do well on cameras. I am so happy for all of you- you must be so relieved. Mary Jane, if you ever need to talk or anything, you have my number."

Jacki darted out the side door of the courthouse and headed for her car. She was surprising Susie at school and dismissing her early to spend the afternoon together. The court proceedings took a little longer than anticipated, but it was still only 1:30 in the afternoon. She drove to the school excited to be with her little sister for the afternoon. Donna had the idea and asked Jacki if she'd be willing to pull it off. She found a parking space a short walking distance away from the sight of any classroom windows, unsure of which class Susie was currently in. Jacki walked into the main office and was greeted by Daphne, the school receptionist. "Hello! Welcome to our school. How can I help you today?" "My name is Jacki Redmund. I'm here to dismiss Susie early for the day." Daphne smiled. "So, you're the big sister Susie can't stop talking about. It's a pleasure to finally meet you. And thank you for all you did behind the scenes. Susie tells everyone who will listen how her new big sister Jacki saved her and got her back in school with her buddies." Jacki smiled. The thought of hearing Susie share that story warmed her heart. "Well, she's special to me, too. Her mom set this up and I am excited to pull it off." Daphne pulled up Susie's schedule and dialed the classroom phone number. A few minutes later, Susie walked into the office with a petrified look on her face. That face melted into pure joy when she turned and saw Jacki in the corner.

"Jacki! What are you doing here?" Jacki laughed. "Surprising you, goof nut! You're done with school for the day and we're going out to lunch and whatever else we can think of." The excitement on Susie's face was priceless. She threw her backpack at Jacki and went running for the door, without even saying goodbye to Daphne. "Hey! Don't I get a goodbye hug?" Daphne called out. Susie giggled as she ran back to Daphne. "You go have fun now. I wish my sister was this fun!" Daphne waved as Jacki and Susie left the building. "First up is lunch, I'm starving" Jacki said as she threw Susie's backpack in the back seat. "Where are we going?" Susie asked. "I wondered why my mom didn't pack me lunch today. I thought maybe she just forgot." Jacki laughed. "Nope. We had this planned for a couple weeks now. Where do you want to go?" They chose Maggie Mae's, their favorite hangout down by the lake. It was too chilly to eat at the lake, so they enjoyed a nice window view instead. Jacki had her usual ravioli dish, while Susie went for chicken tenders.

"How was school today?" Jacki asked, as they waited for their food. "Do you like being back with your friends?"

"School was good. Some of my friends don't talk to me anymore, but the ones that do are so happy I am back. We're learning about President Kennedy in History class."

"I loved that unit when I was in school. My history teacher, Mrs. Rift, was so great at teaching it. Made us feel like we were there on the streets watching it. My dad would always tell me he named me after Jackie Kennedy but wanted me to have my own identity so took off the e at the end."

"How was your day, Jacki?" Susie asked. "It's been a while since I saw you."

Jacki sighed. She didn't want to weigh Susie down with the events of her past few shifts, but Susie was intuitive, so lying or holding back was not an option. "It's been a rough couple of days, but that makes this moment all the more special." "What's wrong, Jacki?" Susie asked, picking up on Jacki's hidden emotions.

"Just had some difficult experiences. I had to baptize two babies that were born into heaven. That was hard because it reminded me of my own baby I lost." Susie looked up at Jacki. "You lost a baby? That's so sad, Jacki. You would be a great mom." Jacki swallowed a lump that had formed in her throat, caught off guard by the emotions of Susie's words. "I did. She wasn't fully developed yet, but she was my baby girl. I named her Melanie. It's been a few years, now, but it still hurts now and then."

"What do you do…when it hurts?" Susie asked. Jacki sighed. "It depends. Sometimes I just let it pass. It doesn't always hurt, sometimes it's a happy thought. But when it hurts, I usually go to a special place in the hospital. The nursery. I look at the babies, I let my mind wander. It's almost like picking something off a shelf, touching it and holding it, and putting it back."

Susie looked down at the table with a sad, concerned look on her face. "You said you can't have babies, right? So, you can't get pregnant again and have another baby?" Jacki shook her head. "That's right, Susie. Not that having another baby would ever replace Melanie, but, no, I cannot have any other babies. My body doesn't let me carry them to a healthy point. It is very hard to accept, but I'm working on it." Jacki paused for a moment. To change the subject, she decided to tell Susie about her upcoming promotion "I do have some good news though. I am going to be promoted to Director of Spiritual Care in July." Susie's special smile reappeared. "That is awesome, Jacki! You are good at your job. I'm so glad we met." Jacki paid their bill and they headed for the car. "So, what should we do next? Any ideas?"

"Let's go bowling!" Susie exclaimed. Jacki laughed. "Alright, bowling it is! But it must be the 10-pin balls, I can't do those New England Candlepins to save my life. And then after bowling, let's go see a movie. Winner picks." "You're on!" Susie said excitedly. Jacki headed to the bowling alley. It had been close to 20 years since Jacki last bowled. "I used to have the highest average on my high school team, you know," she said to Susie. "Well, then it should be a good game." Susie snapped back in a challenging tone. They played three games, and Susie won the first two. The third one went to Jacki, but that meant Susie picked the movie. "Since I'm the winner, let's go see a play instead of a movie!" They ended up going to the theater to see the high school version of Sound of Music. The actors were great, and Susie enjoyed herself. Jacki did too. She decided to take the long way home, so they could hit Jacki's favorite ice cream stand. "No sister date night is complete without an ice cream cone" Jacki said, as she pulled into the parking lot. Susie got vanilla and Jacki went with her favorite, black raspberry. They drove back to Donna's house and parked outside, neither of them wanting the evening to end. "This was so much fun, Jacki. I hope we can do it again. Maybe a sleepover."

"I would love that, Susie. I really enjoyed our time together. It's been a stressful week, but this time with you made me stop and relax. I will be in touch to plan that sleepover." They shared a hug before Susie went inside. Donna waved from the second-floor window as Jacki drove away. Driving back to her house, Jacki reflected on the events of the day. And how grateful she was to have a job that allowed her to make connections with ordinary people. People that would become friends and sisters. Hospital chaplains see a lot of traumas. They see people in their last moments, and in moments of darkness. But sometimes, the light a chaplain brings can change their lives and shine light on a path that otherwise would remain dark.

Chapter 13

Jacki's shift was uneventful for the first half of the morning. She had her usual assignments on the psychiatric and SUD units, made a few referrals for treatment, and visited other patients on the floors who requested spiritual care visits. She had all her rounds completed by 10 that morning, so decided to take a stroll through the Palliative Care unit. Oh boy. A comfort cart outside a doorway is always a somber sight, Jacki thought to herself. She said hello to the receptionist, a new person she hadn't met before, and made a mental note to introduce herself on her way back through. None of the patients requested Spiritual care, but Jacki decided to knock on the door of the patient whose family was gathered, to see if they needed anything. A lovely red-headed lady answered the knock on the door. It was clear that she had been crying. "Hello, I'm Jacki, the hospital chaplain. I noticed the comfort cart outside the door while making my rounds and thought I would check to see if anybody needed anything." The young lady sniffled and opened the door. "Come in. That was nice of you. Our grandma is actively passing. She requested her family to be around her, so we're all here, minus a few of the grandchildren that couldn't make it out in time. We're scattered around the country." The rest of the family looked up as Jacki entered. "This is the hospital chaplain" the lady said. "She was doing her rounds and saw that we were gathered and offered to come and check on us." A man stood up and offered his hand. "I'm Peter. Thank you for stopping by. Our priest is out of town on a family vacation with his siblings, so your visit is perfect timing." He went around the room, introducing his entire family. When he stopped at the young lady that answered the door, she took over and introduced herself instead. "And I'm Colleen. I should have introduced myself earlier when I answered the door." Jacki took her hand and smiled. "No worries at all. You had more important things on your mind. I hope I didn't interrupt anything."

"Not at all!" Peter exclaimed. "She is pretty much unconscious at this point. She moves around on occasion, makes noises. But we promised her we'd all be here when dad came to get her, so we will sit and talk amongst each other and remember the good times." Jacki smiled. "I love to hear that. As a hospital chaplain, I have seen far too many families who do not understand the death process. They think if they're unconscious that they can't hear anything or they leave the bedside because they feel bored or silly. Your mother can hear you, and I'm sure although she can't show it, or speak her thoughts, she loves the fact that you are together and remembering the many memories you had. Those memories will live on and continue to sustain you through the difficult moments." Jacki stepped back and observed for a few moments. Suddenly, the patient started breathing heavily. Some family members reacted with love and care towards their mother, while others were scared. "Is she in pain?" Colleen asked. "No," Jacki said. "It may look very uncomfortable, but she is being kept comfortable with her morphine. The fact she is unconscious is also helpful. It is more painful for us to watch than it is for her. She is not in any pain at all."

Peter stood by his mother's bedside, holding her hand with the loving touch of a son dedicated to his mother. He suddenly looked up at Jacki. "Are hospital chaplains allowed to give last rites? This all happened so suddenly, and our priest is out of town."

"Unfortunately, we are not allowed to give the actual sacrament of last rites. However, I can say prayers with you. I assure you that although last rites are important for Catholic families, there are many who pass without it, and I'm sure they still reach their heavenly destinations. We usually have an on-call priest if you'd prefer. I can tell the charge nurse to have him paged." Peter thought for a moment and then shook his head. "The prayers will do fine. We just want our faith to be part of this moment somehow. Our mom is special to us, and raised us Catholic, but not the Catholics you see in the world. We were raised to never feel more important than anyone else. We were raised on compassion, not on judgement and condemning others for believing or acting differently." Jacki nodded. "I understand. If the family is ready, we can gather and say prayers together." Everyone agreed and joined hands to pray around their mother and grandmother. "What is your mother's name?" Peter chuckled. "That would be helpful, wouldn't it. Her name is Aliette. We're French in case you haven't figured that one out." Jacki laughed. "Yeah, I gathered that, apart from Colleen's name. That one threw me off for a moment." Colleen smiled. Jacki began praying for the peace of Aliette's soul, and for comfort for her family as they grieved the loss of their mother. She encouraged each family member to prayerfully share their goodbye's, and then ended with the Our Father. She laid hands on Aliette's, praying for a peaceful passing free of pain and suffering. A few minutes later, as Jacki was preparing to leave, the family noticed her breathing had stopped. "That is exactly how I wanted her to go," Peter said, wiping away a tear. "It's like she just slipped away before us, into dad's arms. They were ballroom dancers." Jacki took a moment to imagine that visual and smiled. "That's a comforting image you just created for your family. I'm so sorry for your loss. I'm glad I was here to help, and it was a pleasure to meet you all. I know you said your priest is away but if you are having a non-church service, hospital chaplains can perform funeral services and I'd be honored to." Peter shook his head gently. "That is very kind of you. Our church does have a priest that is filling in for funerals and weekend services, but we're an old-fashioned French family that is observing the all-day wake tradition at the funeral home, if you would be willing to come and pray with those in attendance, and perhaps say a few words." Jacki agreed and gave them her card, asking them to just let her know when and where and she would come and share a few words of comfort and pray with them. She was leaving when Colleen called her name and followed her out. "What's up, Colleen? Do you need something?"

"I just wanted to talk to you for a moment. About your job. I'm a senior in high school and I'm really considering being a hospital chaplain. I've always wanted to serve people when they need it most. When you knocked at the door and said you were the chaplain, I just had to ask." Jacki smiled and gave Colleen one of her business cards. "I'm glad to see someone so young interested, and I'm not saying this to discourage you, but it's not for everyone. Reach out to me sometime next week, I'll see if I can schedule a job shadow for you. If, after shadowing me, you still feel like this is where you're being led, we can talk about next steps, as I'm sure you're curious as to what the school requirements are." Colleen thanked Jacki and went back in to be with her family. The nurse had just gone in to confirm that she had passed. She stopped on her way out to introduce herself to the receptionist, but she was away from the desk, so Jacki headed for the cafeteria. She didn't realize it was lunch time until she had stepped out of the room and into the hallway.

She scanned the weekly menu, but nothing enticed her, so she opted for the sandwich line. She ordered a roast beef wrap and grabbed a serving of French fries. After paying for her lunch, she headed over to where Sara was sitting. "Hey, girl. How goes the battle" Jacki said, sitting down.

"Jacki! I didn't even see you come in! It's unusually simple in the ED today. I'm almost afraid that something big is going to happen. How's your day going?"

"Mine's been rather simple, too, honestly. I had all my rounds done by 10, so went up to the Palliative Care unit. I saw a comfort cart outside of a door, so once I checked with the other patients, I knocked on that door. Ended up staying with the family until their mom passed. It was special to see an old-fashioned family all gathered around their loved one. Her granddaughter, Colleen asked me about being a hospital chaplain. I'll check with Kathryn and see if I can schedule a shadow. I was surprised you don't see many young people interested in this job. Nursing, yes, chaplaincy, not so much."

"Well, perhaps they see the light you are spreading, and want a piece of that. You make a big difference, Jacki. Rather you want to admit it or not. Are you going to the awards banquet? What are you wearing?" *That's an odd change of subjects,* Jacki thought to herself.

"I am. I'm not sure what I'm wearing yet. I'm planning to go shopping with Sandie over the weekend. I hate dress shopping, even more so when it must be the fancy dresses."

"I'm sure you'll find the perfect dress. I'm wearing my red dress I got for my sister's wedding last year. I'm excited, it'll be nice to be together with other co-workers from all over the hospital and celebrate with those that win awards."

"Yeah, I highly doubt I'll win one, but with Kathryn, I've learned to expect the unexpected. But I must say I'm looking forward to it, too. I'm bringing Susie as my guest. Alisha's

invited, too, apparently because she and Sandie are both going."
Jacki noticed that Sara had started to comment and then stopped
herself. Although she was curious, she decided to let it go. They
talked about church service on Sunday and doing lunch afterward
and were just about finished their lunch when the intercom
sprang to life: Trauma Activation. ED. Trauma Activation. ED.
Critical Care Team activated.

"Uh oh!" Sara and Jacki said in unison, as they quickly threw their
garbage away and ran down the stairs and buzzed into the ED just
as the ambulance was rolling in. Sara took one side, while Jacki
stood on the other. "What do we have, boys?" Sara asked the
paramedics. "50-year-old male. One vehicle car accident. Serious
traumatic injuries. Semi-conscious." Jacki stepped out, partially
to let the medical team do their jobs, but also because she knew
who that man on the gurney was. She closed her eyes and prayed:
God, help me to be merciful to Father Thomas. He has not been
the greatest example of compassion when I and many of his
parishioners have needed him. But now he needs compassion
and mercy himself. Bless the hands who will attempt to save his
life and I thank you for the strength you'll give me to minister to
him in his time of need.

Jacki had forgiven Father Thomas for the hurt she caused her
when she lost Melanie. But seeing him unexpectedly brought

back all those moments and all the pain. She did not plan on sharing her experience with him, as she was never one to bring up old hurts. He, if he survived, would no doubt have his own stories to share, and she intended to listen to him and minister to him in that moment. For now, however, she retreated to the chapel until his condition was more known.

Jacki hadn't heard anything about Father Thomas's condition, so she decided to check with Sara. "I'm sorry, Jacki. It's been so busy that I forgot to keep you updated. He was moved upstairs; he's alert and talking. He's lucky. He had a lot of internal damage, but luckily none of it was fatal. Few more minutes though, and things might have been different."

Although Jacki was dreading this conversation with him, she was glad to hear he would be alright. Suffering from injuries that severe is not something she would wish on anyone. "What floor is he on? Med-Surg?"

"ICU-N, he's on step down status but they're waiting for a bed to move him to. Do you know him? He seemed afraid once he found out you were the chaplain." Jacki nodded her head. "Sounds about right. I'll explain later." Jacki headed up the stairs. She needed the exercise as a distraction. This conversation would not be easy. The receptionist smiled at Jacki on her way by. ICU-N was a busy unit, with lots of patient transport to the other floors pending. Jacki smiled back and found Father Thomas's room and knocked on the door. "Come in, Jacki. I knew you'd be visiting." *At least he knows my name,* she thought to herself. "Hi Father Thomas. What a surprise to see you here. I'm so sorry for your accident. I heard you are very lucky to still be with us."

"Thank you, Jacki." He said, as he pointed to a chair. 'Sit. Please. I've been waiting for your visit."

"Why is that?" Jacki asked, curious as to why he'd be looking forward to seeing her.

"I hope you never have to experience what I did, but serious accidents like this can cause people to have experiences where their lives flash before their eyes. I had that experience, only I saw my priesthood flash before my eyes."

Jacki shifted in her chair, unsure of where this was going or what exactly he wanted from her. She decided to just let him share. "I haven't been a good priest, Jacki. To you, especially, but also to so many others. The many people I've judged for things that I shouldn't have. I denied your precious child a funeral service because of something minor, I made you feel worse when you came to me for comfort in the aftermath of your loss. I told people they couldn't take communion because of a divorce; I've judged people based on things I shouldn't have. I was not being Christ at all, I was placing my own opinions and views on others, instead of guiding them in the way of Christ." To Jacki's surprise, he started to cry. Jacki took a breath before speaking to him. "You did hurt me, Father Thomas. The hurt you caused does surface at times, and I still struggle with grieving my child because of what was said and done. But I have forgiven you, father. You are human after all. I can't speak for the others that you've hurt, or condemned, or driven away. I don't have a real answer to give you. All I can suggest, is to try to use this recovery period as a sabbatical and use it to become a better priest once you return to ministry. You have a long road ahead of you. You recognized your mistakes, while other priests I'm sure are too blinded by their own opinions to notice."

Father Thomas looked at Jacki with tears in his eyes. "Thank you, for your forgiveness, Jacki. I am deeply sorry that I hurt you. I'm sorry that your child did not get a memorial service because of my selfishness. I know how important that is to someone's grief journey."

"I appreciate that. It made grieving difficult, to not have the closure to say goodbye. Luckily, the church I attend now was willing to do a service after the fact. It was attended by the few friends I had in my corner at the time, plus members of the Women's Ministry that came to support me. She's buried with my father. Like you, I have a long way to go in healing, and I will never be truly healed until I'm reunited with her and my father. It is difficult to know I cannot have another child. I will not sugar coat it, father, your words hurt me in that instance. I chose to leave the church because of your words and the alleged doctrines you told me supported your beliefs."

Father Thomas smiled. "Well, something wonderful did come out of such a sad moment, then, because you found Christ in a new way, and from what I hear you are an amazing chaplain. I also heard through the grapevine that you are going to be the Director of Spiritual Care comes the summer. That is truly amazing, Jacki."

"Thank you, father. It was not easy for me to leave the faith I had known for so long. But, with what you told me in the moment, as well as other beliefs that I struggled with, I had to go and find the Jesus that is in the bible, who loves everyone and doesn't call anyone a failure, or condemn them for things beyond their control. I found a faith that lets me serve as a chaplain, without the stigma and expectation of upholding the Catholic teachings."

"I am happy for you, Jacki. And I am grateful that I got to be a recipient of your ministry today. I do hope you will come back to visit me. I am sure I will be here for a while. I am proud of you, Jacki. I caused you to have a horrible experience, on top of the tragedy you were already dealing with. But you took it and let God guide you to a place where you could heal and use the gifts, he's given you to help others. Go and do good work, Jacki. Our church's loss is countless people's blessing." Father Thomas gave Jacki a blessing, before she left. While she was in this area of the hospital, she stopped by to talk with Kathryn about Colleen. Jacki knocked on the door before entering.

"Hi Jacki. How did things go with Father Thomas? I know that was not easy."

"It went better than I thought it would," Jacki said, plopping down on the couch. "He apologized to me, which is something I thought I would never get. He admitted he was a priest led by his own opinions and views, and not the teachings and views he should have been preaching."

"Wow. That's a blessing. I hope he does something with it."

"Me, too. I suggested he take this time of recovery to refocus and work on himself, spend time in prayer. And when he returns to ministry, be the priest he wanted to be but never was. But, anyway, I'm here for a different reason."

Kathryn put her pencil down. "You're not here to tell me you decided not to take the promotion, are you?" Jacki rolled her eyes. "Of course not. I am excited about that to be honest. I ran into someone while visiting a patient in the Palliative Care unit. Her name's Colleen, she's a senior in high school and has an interest in chaplaincy. I was wondering if it would be alright for her to do a job shadow with me one day." Kathryn's eyes beamed with excitement. "Someone that young interested in spiritual care in a hospital setting. That's a rarity. Absolutely!"

"Perfect!" Jacki said excitedly. "She's a lovely young lady, I can tell just by the way she stood around her grandmother, that she has such compassion and gentleness. Perhaps we can discuss doing an internship over the summer as well. I could supervise her."

"Look at you go, miss Director! It'll be your call by then, you do what you feel would work for her."

"Thanks, Kathryn. I just wanted to run it by you first. I know everything will be under my leadership by the summer, but I still feel I must run things by my superior."

"Totally understandable." Kathryn said with a smile. "I'm glad you stopped by. Here's your invitation to the awards banquet. I'm sure you were planning on going anyways, but you're getting a hand delivered invitation, so you must be there." Jacki sighed. She was not a fan of fancy events. "Why does this feel the same to me as being summoned to a court hearing." Jacki said sarcastically. "I hate going dress shopping. But it's been a while since I've had to wear one, so I suppose I'm about due to dress up."

Kathryn frowned. She hated to hear Jacki talk about herself like that. But she knew bits and pieces of her upbringing, which wasn't very supportive. Knowing what she did made her even more grateful that Mount Mercy was able to hire her and let her shine. They talked for a few more minutes, before Jacki headed back to her assignment sheets.

She texted Colleen and let her know the job shadow would be okay, and that she would reach out another time to determine a good day that worked for her, then went and continued with her assignments. Her assigned floors were quiet, so she floated onto the labor & delivery floor. Sometimes Jacki would walk through the unit just to be on a happy floor. While she loved her job, there were days where endless tragedy and loss took its toll. To hear a baby's cry or see someone become a parent for the first time put a smile on her face, despite the deep longing for it to be her turn and knowing it never could be. She stopped at the nursery window, the place she went when she needed to visit her own wounded heart. After a few minutes, Jacki sighed and walked away. She swung through the ED one final time before clocking out and headed home for a quiet night with her dog. She was off this weekend. She made plans with Sandie to go dress shopping, and decided a new suit for Jeffrey's upcoming trial would be a good idea. Thankfully, she was not testifying in that trial, but would attend the entire trial as a show of support for Jeffrey and his family.

Chapter 14

Jacki had made plans with Sandie to go shopping, but not until 10, so, for the first time in a while, she opted not to set her alarm and let her body wake up when it was ready. She was still surprised when her eyes finally awoke, and it was already eight! She hopped out of bed, fed her dog, and then took her out for her morning walk. She made breakfast and then took her shower, leaving her just enough time to get to Sandie's house. They were taking Sandie's car because it was easier than taking two cars, with all the stores they were planning on going to. Jacki pulled in next to Sandie's car just as Sandie was heading outside.

"Good timing!" Sandie said. "Ready for a day of shopping?"

"As I'll ever be" Jacki sighed. "You know how much I hate dress shopping. It always makes me feel fat."

Sandie gave her a look of disgust. "You are NOT fat, young lady. What your mother told you was a flat out lie. You may not be a size 2, but why would you want to be that thin. You must learn to love the body God gave you, Jacki. You're a beautiful woman, and the clothes you wear can allow people to see the beauty inside of you, as well as what's on the outside."

"I know," Jacki said in a hushed tone. "It just seems like all the pretty dresses I would love to wear don't come in my size. The ones I can pick from are not as fancy, and always dark colors. Or have deep necklines."

Sandie agreed with her on that one. "Well, we're going to a store that specializes in real clothing sizes, it's a long drive, but I think you'll enjoy the selection."

"We're starting with coffee first, I hope" Jacki said with a laugh. About an hour later, they arrived at a store with so many dresses Jacki didn't know where to start. Sandie was right, these were real dresses, pretty dresses, in real sizes. The store attendant came over almost as soon as they walked in.

"Hi! My name is Emily. Can I help you find something today?" the young lady said with a smile.

"I have an awards banquet for work at the end of June, and I'm not the best dress shopper. I have no idea what colors look good on me, or what types of dresses I like. I'm a horrible client, just to warn you." Emily laughed. "Oh, I've had enough stories to make your hair curl, you are the least of my worries. Let's start with a simple question---do you want long or short?"

Jacki thought for a moment. "I would love a long one, but with my height, it's not an easy fit. I don't want to disappear under the dress." Emily stepped back, as if she was getting a visual of Jacki in her mind, to take to the many selections. "Perhaps a nice mid-length, then. Mid-lengths always look long on the shorter people. Let's step this way." The store seemed never ending with a wide selection of colors, fabrics, designs, and occasions. When they finally got to the mid-length section, Jacki was still amazed at the selection.

"Now comes the hard part. What's your favorite color? What colors do you enjoy wearing?"

Jacki sighed. She felt like dress shopping was just as painful as peeling off layers of an onion. "My favorite color is yellow, but I also have been told the sapphire or royal blue's look good on me. My mother would tell me since I wasn't thin, I could only wear dark colors, so I don't wear very much for color."

Emily frowned. "I'm so sorry. That's horrible for a mother to say. Everyone can wear colors, regardless of their sizes. Let's try some on and see what you like."

Jacki and Sandie looked through the large selection, pulling out styles and designs she liked. She then started the tedious process of elimination by trying on each dress. A few, due to the style and fabric, did not fit in her usual size choice, so were easily eliminated. By the time they were finished, Jacki had narrowed it down to three, and tried them on again. She ultimately decided to step outside of her comfort triangle and went with a magenta dress with sequined sleeves. The skirt portion of the dress resembled a hi-low fashion, where it was longer in the back than the front, which Jacki wore often. Luck would have it that the dress was also on sale, allowing Jacki to find a few more dressy pantsuits to wear for Jeffrey's trial, and work.

"Well, that went smoother than I thought" Jacki said to Sandie as they walked out the door.

"I told you this place was the best! Lara wasn't as thin as she was recently. We bought her prom dresses here. We love it here."

"Have a favorite place to eat around here, too?" Jacki asked. "It is lunch time after all."

"As a matter of fact, I already have reservations made. There's an Italian place not too far from here that has the most unique pasta selections around. You like Italian, right?"

Jacki snickered. "Is the Pope Catholic? Heck yes, I LOVE Italian!" They both laughed as they drove. There appeared to be an accident up ahead which was making traffic travel at a snail's pace. Jacki didn't mind. She enjoyed time with Sandie and their conversations always ended up meaningful. But she had a feeling this one was going to turn on her and enter a new level of special.

"So, how's the rest of your week been? Did you save anymore lives?"

Jacki laughed. "Saving lives is not exactly what I do, but I suppose you could say I help save souls, by listening to the patient's needs. It's been an oddly uneventful week, to be honest. Yesterday I had most of my assigned floors done, so strolled onto the Palliative Care unit and ended up tending bedside with a wonderful French family. Their mother was actively passing, well into her 90s. Everyone was there that lived close enough. One of her granddaughters, Colleen, is interested in hospital spiritual care work, so I'm going to plan a job shadow day with her in a couple weeks."

"I am so impressed to see more women entering the Spiritual Care world. It's always been almost off-limits unless you were a priest or pastor, or a religious sister. But lately it seems to be picking up interest." Jacki agreed. "It's picking up speed, for sure. I feel it's some kind of spiritual care revival. People are realizing the importance of total wellness, including one's spiritual side. Colleen is so compassionate; I think she'll be great in this field. We will see what she thinks after her job shadow."

"Did you hear about that horrible accident yesterday? They said the driver was lucky to be alive."

Jacki nodded. "That's for sure. Father Thomas Finnigan was that driver. He is very lucky to be alive. He seems to be stabilizing well, though. I spoke with him yesterday."

Sandie paused and looked at Jacki, before turning her attention back to the traffic in front of them. "Isn't that the priest that was at your church when you lost Melanie? I remember Alisha telling me how much of a hard time he gave you."

Jacki sighed. "Yes, he was horrible to me at that time. It's a big piece of what drove me out of that faith, the words he used. Once I walked away from the situation, I was able to forgive him. But his words still echo in my mind often. It's been a big hurdle in my grieving Melanie. Feeling like I have no right to grieve, because according to him, she has no value. If she didn't breathe on this earth, that was meant to happen, she was destined to die and therefore has no value." Sandie's grip tightened on the steering wheel; Jacki could tell she was mad.

"He said that to you. Goodness, Jacki. I'm so sorry. That is not true! I hope you've come to realize that."

"I have. It's been a painful journey, but I'm getting there. Visting her the other day helped greatly. I let out a lot of emotions just sitting with her. And talking with him helped, too. He admitted he was wrong, and that he wronged many other parishioners with his words and thoughts."

"I just can't understand how a priest can say those things and attempt to back them up with doctrines. I remember Alisha being so mad when you shared with her what had happened."

Jacki laughed. "Oh yes, mad is putting it lightly. If I didn't know her as well as I do, I'd think she would have gone and beat him up for me. I don't know what made him say what he did either, but he admitted he used that method with a lot of people in the past. He let himself get in the way. I told him perhaps he should take the recovery time as a sabbatical and really press into God's Word, find strength to overcome whatever it is he's struggling with inside, and become the priest he wasn't before."

"You are so wise, Jacki. You're right. I always say life doesn't come with a delete button, but it does come with a backspace. Sometimes things happen in our lives to wake us up and begin again."

There was a silence in the car for a few minutes that seemed like forever to Jacki. But she didn't know how to fill the silence. Suddenly, the traffic lightened up after they passed the accident. The rest of the ride went by quickly and they pulled into the restaurant. Once they were seated, Sandie pulled out a small gift.

"What is this for?" Jacki asked, taking the small package.

"Just something I saw that made me think of you. I hope you like it."

Curious, Jacki opened the small box, to find an ornament with a sleeping baby in the center. The name plate read "Melanie". Jacki was completely caught off guard, to the point where tears began sliding down her face.

"Sandie----it's beautiful. When I lost Melanie, Christmas was always so hard for me. Because I felt I couldn't honor her in any way. There'd never be anything with her name on it---no stockings, no gifts. Everybody was there for me in the beginning, but when I struggled longer than a few months, when I still spoke about her after the first year---they disappeared. They told me I was stuck, that I should just move on and find something else to fill that space."

Sandie took Jacki's hand and looked at her. "Well---you're not stuck. You're a grieving mother. Rather they like it or not, rather they accept her as a child or not—she is your child. Nothing, and when I say nothing, I mean nothing, will ever fill that space. I lost Jacob and had Lara shortly after. Did having other children help? Absolutely. But it never completely went away. It's not supposed to. That child is yours from the moment its life begins. If it doesn't get to stay long, its absence is felt forever. Like any wound, it will heal on the outside, but on the inside---the scars, the rawness…all of that is always going to be there. Just at the surface, waiting to be activated. I wish I had known you then, Jacki. If I did, I would have never walked away from you, like everyone else did. I promise you now, I'll never walk away. You can come to me whenever you're missing Melanie, whenever you need to talk about her."

"Now I see why you found us a table in a far-off corner." Jacki said, wiping her eyes with a napkin. "Thank you. That's exactly what I feel like right now. I've healed a lot, or so I thought. I've had to face so many triggers the past few weeks and being there for you with Lara…it just brought everything to the surface again. Having to see Father Thomas was the icing on the cake. Alisha was there for me at that moment, and for that I'm so grateful. Now I have you. And Melanie can always be a part of my Christmas tree, thanks to her grandma Sandie thinking of her."

Their food arrived shortly after. "These are the best stuffed shells I've had!" Jacki exclaimed. "And the fact they have different flavors is amazing."

"Told you, I know Italian when I see it. It's a bit of a trip, but it's worth it for the great food and service."

Although it was tempting, Sandie and Jacki opted to bypass dessert and head back home. They were about halfway home when they hit another accident backup.

"I guess we're just meant to spend time together today" Sandie said with a laugh. "Or we have a bad sense of direction, one of the two."

Jacki laughed. "I'll go with option A. I'm in no rush to get home if you're not. After the emotional lunch we had, having some down time to wait in traffic isn't a bad idea." They let the silence linger for a few minutes, listening to music. A song played on the radio that meant a lot to Alisha.

"One of Alisha's first hospice patients loved this song" Sandie said. "Now, every time it plays, we think of him." Jacki nodded. She remembered that story well. She allowed herself to get lost in the song. Once it ended, she turned to Sandie. "Do you have a song that makes you think of Jacob? Or Lara?" Sandie shook her head. "Not really. Different circumstances, but my grief journey with Jacob was a lot like yours. There's a song my church plays at Eastertime that makes me think of them because of the melody. It's peaceful and lighthearted. Jacki nodded. "Yeah, same with Melanie. I don't have any specific song that makes me think of her. But I think of her a lot when I sing worship songs, because she loved when I'd sing. I swear she knew when it was my Sunday to lead. She'd be so active the entire time. Sometimes when I lead now, I think of her, I miss feeling her moving around so happily. It sounds so stupid. It's been over five years; you'd think I'd forget about feeling her move by now."

Sandie glanced over at her. "Nothing about your journey is ever stupid, Jacki. It is what makes you feel connected to her. If it doesn't bring you into a point of depression, embrace those moments. I know you said the nursery window brings you comfort at times, too. Do what you need to do. This is your journey, nobody else's. I can walk it with you, but I can't tell you to do it one way or another. You do what brings you comfort, even if others don't understand. They should be grateful they don't have to understand." Jacki nodded as she stared out the window, attempting to hide the fact that she was about to start crying again. Sandie sensed her emotions and reached for her hand. "Don't hide your emotions, missy. It's okay to cry in this car. In my home. If there are tears, it means love lived there first. To hold that love in would be an insult to Melanie." Jacki wiped her tears away. "I know. It's just hard to remember that I'm with someone that won't turn on me and tell me to stop. I've come so far, or so I thought. Maybe I haven't gotten anywhere, just learned to store up all the emotions like a storage unit."

Sandie nodded. "Yes. It's a lot easier to just stack all our emotions into those storage units and lock the door, isn't it? We think they're safe there, and we look like we have it all together. Nobody can tell from the outside what's in those storage units. Sometimes, we fill them so much that we don't even let Jesus into them. He sends us people to help unload those storage units. They're called friends. Real friends. I'm here, Jacki. Let me in. I'll help you sort through all the stuff you have in there." Jacki's tears were falling freely now. And for once, she did not care. She found Sandie's hand and just held it, allowing the tears to fall. When she finally felt she could speak again, she turned to Sandie. "Thank you. There's just so much in there. I have a good relationship with God, I give him all these things, I know he's in control. But it's just so hard dealing with all of this by myself. So, I cry, I have my moment and then I lock it away. I have a counselor, but she's not there the moment a trigger happens. There are years, Sandie, years of grief, guilt, heartache, emptiness, anger, shattered dreams. I don't know where to start."

"Right where you are, Jacki." Sandie said encouragingly. "The first step is the most important. You do have it all together, your patients would never know. And sometimes, especially in the work field you are in, that's a good thing. But you need to make sure you're also healing from within. I think these past few weeks have put the key into the lock and jiggled it, and that's why it hurts. Melanie wouldn't want you to hold onto her in a negative way. Your love for her shines brightly. It's time you let that light shine, instead of hiding it under a mask to make everyone else comfortable. You speak to others every day of the importance of mercy, forgiving themselves and others, you're compassionate towards them in sorrows…don't forget to give yourself that same treatment. You're not alone anymore."

The traffic lightened up almost immediately after their conversation ended. Jacki looked over with a smile. "I guess

Melanie wanted us to have that conversation before the traffic lightened."

"I was thinking the same thing" Sandie said. "And we are coming up on an ice cream place, so I think she wants ice cream, too." They both laughed as they got out of the car to get an ice cream cone to end their emotional day. "Good thing I can burn this all off before the banquet, or else that dress we just bought may not fit."

"It's got room to be let out if necessary. That's still a good four months away, girl. Eat the dang ice cream!" They both laughed and enjoyed the rest of the afternoon. Jacki felt a difference already, just knowing she no longer had to deal with this by herself. She has a good friend who wants to listen. When she got home, Jacki checked her messages. Colleen was excited to look at schedules for a job shadow day and was looking forward to seeing her tomorrow for her grandmother's wake service. Jacki decided a long, relaxing run was necessary to wind down after such a beautiful, healing day. Then she worked on her message for tomorrow's wake service and headed for an early night.

Jacki woke up at 6:00, showered, walked her dog, and then changed into one of her new pant suits for Aliette's wake service. She drove to the funeral home, where Pete was once again working. "Hello, stranger" he said, as he opened the door for Jacki.

"Well, hello. We really need to stop meeting like this." They both laughed.

"How's things since the last time I saw you" Pete asked.

"Pretty good, actually. Lots of difficult cases, but overall, I love my job. You never know who you will be ministering to. I will be taking over the Director of Spiritual Care position at the end of June, so you probably won't see me as often once I take on more responsibilities at the hospital."

"Jacki! That's amazing! I'm so happy for you. I know things haven't been easy for you the past few years, but things seem to be changing for you. I'm sure I'll still see you, though. A good chaplain never says no to patients that touch their heart." They spoke for a few more minutes, until she saw Colleen in the corner. "I'm going to head in. Colleen is in the hallway. Catch you later." She walked over and hugged Colleen.

"Again, I'm so sorry for your loss. You seemed close with your grandmother." Colleen nodded, wiping away a tear. "It wasn't always this loving. Our family has done a lot of healing over the past few years. I think that's why everyone is taking it so hard, is that we had just recently reconciled as a family, and now she's gone." Jacki nodded. "The important thing, though, is that you did reconcile. Not every family gets that opportunity. Before we go inside, I wanted to let you know that my supervisor gave permission to set up a job shadow. Are you free to come on Friday? It's my last day before I take a few days off, Fridays are usually calm, which would be good for a shadow day."

"That's exciting. Yes, I'm free on Friday. I took the week off from school for bereavement. What time does your shift start?" Jacki quickly pulled out her phone. "11. But I'm usually there early, if you wanted to get there at 10:30, I could meet you in the cafeteria and we could grab a coffee before we start."

"Sounds great! Thanks again, Jacki." They went into the chapel together, where Colleen ushered her through a long line of extended family members and friends. A few minutes later the prayer service began with the soothing sounds of a piano player. A few minutes later, Colleen's father stood up to introduce Jacki.

"While our mother was in her final hours, a wonderful hospital chaplain came into the room. She wasn't assigned to our mother's case but stayed with us anyway. She was there at the time our beloved mother passed away, offering to pray with us in absence of our parish priest. We've invited her here this morning to share a few words of comfort with us. Jacki." At the sound of her name, Jacki approached the podium and began with her typical condolences. She then pulled out a notebook that had her planned words. She looked up and began.

"While I did not know Aliette her entire life, the few hours I spent with her loving family allowed me to know enough of her. The fact that this chapel is nearly packed solid is a testament to the importance of family. Aliette's French heritage meant a lot to her. French families stick together. But we live in a broken world, with broken people. Broken people hurt others. From what I learned through sitting with the family, Aliette has had her share of hurt. The family withstood tragedy, and although they at times were not as amicable, they are all here today. Why? Because Aliette did not give up. Aliette may have been mad for a time, but she forgave. She loved her family enough to overlook the hurt and forgive whatever was done. Jesus showed us how we are to love when he forgave the very people that murdered him, saying 'forgive them, for they know not what they are doing.' No doubt many times, Aliette mumbled those same words. Despite the many hurts, fights, and moments of familial unrest, when Aliette needed her family the most---they were there. They loved her in her final moments. They stood and sat around her, sharing stories of better days. Sharing moments of ballroom dancing with her husband, or the smell of fresh baked bread that every grandchild grew up smelling. They shared photographs, stories, laughs and tears…together. Aliette lived a long life, filled with good and bad times. She loved strongly and fought for what she loved most---her family. And now today, we are all here to gather and remember her. While we may be saddened now, we can take comfort knowing that she is reunited with her husband, dancing an endless waltz with the love of her life, where tears, and pain, illness and disease are no more. And one day, we will too, be united with her, when our time on this earth is done. God bless all of you, as you mourn and remember your mother, grandmother, great-grandmother, sister, cousin, and friend. Well done, Aliette. You have crossed the finish line. You have won the race, now reap your rewards."

When Jacki was finished, she looked around the room to see so many family members wiping tears from their eyes. She found her way to the back of the room and observed for a while. She had never witnessed a French wake in the old tradition before. Colleen found her a few minutes later and handed her a card.

"My father wanted me to give you this, for being with us and offering to speak this morning. That was beautiful, Jacki. She would have loved it, especially that you included her love of dancing." Jacki took the envelope and stuck it inside her notebook. "It was my pleasure. I firmly believe God nudges us to go in certain directions at times. I have many stories to share when we meet on Friday. I was happy to be able to sit with you all in your moment of need. I've never seen one of these wakes before---what makes this tradition so different?"

Colleen laughed. "Well, in the olden days of French families, many families would hold the wakes in their home, so the deceased could feel more at peace in familiar surroundings. Obviously, once embalming became the common practice, this tradition moved to funeral homes. But the tradition really lies with the timing. Most wakes today are only in two-hour increments. So, 2-4 in the afternoon and then 6-8, or 7-9, for example."

"Okay" Jacki nodded in understanding. "So, why are we here at 10 in the morning, then?"

"That is the French tradition---our wakes last all day. Not many families follow that tradition anymore, but my grandmother left it in her living will that she wanted the old-fashioned traditional daylong wake. Hers started at 9, and we won't leave here until 9 or after, depending on how many people are still around at the end."

Jacki's eyes grew wide in disbelief. "TWELVE HOURS? Please tell me you guys eat." Colleen laughed. "Oh yes, Pete makes sure we have snacks within reach, and we do get a lunch and dinner spread in the neighboring gathering space. Like I said, it's a rarity these days but my grandmother wanted it."

"Well, I wish you all the best today. I am sure this will be physically and mentally exhausting for you and your family. And tomorrow is the funeral mass and burial. I'm here if you need me, and I'll see you Friday." They hugged again and Jacki left through the side door, closest to where she parked. She drove home and spent the remainder of the day with her dog, working on her photo album project.

Jacki woke up Friday morning and went through her usual morning routine. Today was going to be a fun day. Colleen was shadowing her for a few hours in the afternoon. She got to the medical center a little earlier than 10:30, to check assignment folders that were left for her and Colleen. Kathryn had changed Jacki's assignment list slightly to better accommodate an intern. She still had the ED to walk through, but instead of her usual floors, Kathryn gave her Palliative Care, Med/Surg and SUD, leaving time for Colleen and Jacki to meet and chat about the experience. She stopped in for a moment to say hi to Kathryn, before organizing her office a bit prior to Colleen's arrival. As soon as she walked into her office, her eyes stumbled upon the basketball Jeffrey had given her. A sentimental mood suddenly came over her, as she walked over and picked up the basketball. As her fingers ran over the bumpy edges, and touched his signature, her mind went to Jeffrey. He was an example of strength. A young boy, coming back from a basketball field trip, suddenly has no legs, his dreams of making it to the big leagues are dashed. Medical advancements may help him in the future, but his life as he knew it was still forever changed. She put the basketball down and reflected on his journey, and how the events of the next week would affect him, and the other students who were injured that day. She was thankful for a job that allowed her to be supportive of her patients and their families well after they left the hospital, even when it came to trials and court proceedings. Her desk phone ringing pulled her out of her thoughts.

"Hello, Jacki speaking."

Jacki was told by the person on the other line that Colleen was waiting in the lobby for her. She glanced at the clock and realized her thoughts had taken her well past the time she was supposed to meet Colleen! "Oh, gee whiz. I'll be right down!" Jacki grabbed the folders and waivers for Colleen and flew down the stairs. She ran so fast, by the time she reached the front desk she was slightly winded. "Colleen I'm so sorry, I got to organizing my office and lost track of time."

"Haha! No worries. Stella here is a stitch. We've been cracking jokes while waiting." Jacki sighed. "Oh, miss Stella certainly is. When she retires, this place will never be the same."

"Excuse me, young lady. I am only 55 and have no intention of going anywhere anytime soon, so you stop that negative talk right this minute!" All three of them laughed. "Thanks for keeping her company, Stella. She's shadowing me today for a couple hours."

Turning to Colleen, Stella said "My apologies ahead of time. Good luck to you!" Again, everyone laughed as Jacki led Colleen around the corner to head for the cafeteria. "I figured we'd start with a tour, get some coffee, have you fill out your forms and then I'll go over our assignments for the afternoon."

"Perfect! I am so excited. Is there someplace I can put my coat and my purse? I think it would get uncomfortable to carry around all afternoon." Jacki laughed. "Agreed. Not to mention some of the floors we're visiting would have to search them. After we grab coffee, I'll stop at my office, and you can leave them there. I'll lock the door, not that anyone ever goes up there. I'll introduce you to Kathryn, too. She's a gem."

Jacki explained the waivers as they found a table in the cafeteria. "These are similar to permission slips, the usual liability stuff, and that you agree not to talk about what you see and what happens, outside of the building." Colleen nodded that she understood and signed all the forms, just as Jacki came back with their coffees. "Now that the boring stuff is over with, ready to start the fun?" "Coffee is transportable, let's do it!" Jacki walked her to the Spiritual Care Department and knocked on Kathryn's door. "It's just me. I wanted to introduce you to Colleen, my job shadow."

"Hello, Colleen. I'm Kathryn. It's nice to meet you. I hope you enjoy your day with Jacki. She tells me you are very compassionate and outgoing."

"Thank you for having me" Colleen replied. "I'm so excited to spend time with Jacki and learn what she does. I know when she knocked on my grandmother's door and simply offered to sit with us, that she was special." Kathryn's eyes sparkled as she smiled. "Oh, special just barely begins to cover it. I didn't choose her to take my position for nothing. I trust her judgement, and really do hope you enjoy it here. Perhaps she'll be able to find you a summer internship if you like it." They talked for a few more minutes, then popped into Jacki's office so Colleen could put her things down. "Nice office, Jacki. I like the color." "Thank you. It's a special color."

As they were headed to the first unit, Jacki explained. "So, a typical day as a chaplain here at Mount Mercy starts with the morning meeting. We all meet in Kathryn's office, and she distributes assignment folders. That's what these things are. If you're regularly assigned to a certain floor, like me being assigned to the ED, you will always get that folder, along with one or two other floors, depending on the staffing."

Colleen looked around at all the sights, as they walked swiftly towards the Med/Surg floor. "The first floor I'm going to take you on is Med/Surg. Before Mount Mercy added the Palliative Care unit, this was the floor our comfort measures patients would be on. Now it's primarily for non-emergent situations that still require hospitalization, such as recovering from surgery, hip, and knee replacements, and FTT's."

"What is an FTT?" Colleen asked. "Failure to Thrive". Those patients are mostly elderly, or developmentally handicapped people that just are not taking care of themselves.

They usually end up being admitted into nursing homes." Colleen nodded. "The first thing we do when we enter a floor is go to the reception desk and grab the roster. Any name that is highlighted is open to a spiritual care visit. Some floors most people are open, while others only have one or two. You stop by each patient that is open to a visit, and let your heart lead the way. You may stay for a few moments, they may be unwell, and not want to talk, or you could be there for an hour sitting with someone who has no visitors." She introduced Colleen to the unit secretary and some of the nurses, then they started working on the rooms. Jacki would introduce Colleen and ask the patients if they were okay with an additional person. A few of them said they'd rather it only be Jacki, so Colleen waited in the hall. "Once you finish all the patients that are highlighted, you return the sheet over here in this box, face down. Each chaplain has a surface for personal notes---this is where they summarize their visit, and if you put in any referrals."

"Why would a chaplain put in a referral? What would it be for?" Colleen asked. "You, as the chaplain, are part of the medical team for each patient. So, if, for example, you're on the Med/Surg floor and you're visiting a new FTT patient, you could put in a referral for social work to have them begin the process for nursing home admittance. Or, on the SUD unit, the chaplain is the one that initiates the paperwork for treatment. We're headed there next."

"Substance Abuse Unit? Is that a thing in every hospital? I've never heard of that!" Jacki smiled. "As a matter of fact, Mount Mercy Medical Center has the only SUD unit in the state. We're hoping eventually it'll become popular enough to reach the other hospitals." They entered the SUD unit and were greeted by Lauryn. "I have some bad news for you, ladies. Our printer is down, so I do not have a list."

"Oh, the joys of technology" Jacki said, rolling her eyes. "Do you mind if I just walk through and show our job shadow Colleen the unit?" "Go for it! Welcome, Colleen. You have a great person showing you the ropes." Jacki smiled. They walked down the hallway, as Jacki pointed out things that you wouldn't see on other units. "All patient medicines are locked up tight on this unit, for obvious reasons. The nurses are the only ones that administer medications on this unit." She pointed out the referral computer unit in the corner, where the chaplain submits the referral. "Other units, you would only talk about the referral in your notes, as the nurses do the physical forms. On the SUD unit, all the referrals are electronic and go right to the designated treatment facility." Jacki pulled up the test referral and had

Colleen fill one in, explaining what each section needed as she did it. "Now hit submit. And Sheilagh over at the treatment center will get this referral." "Wow! That is easy to use compared to some programs. I bet it helps people get into treatment faster, too." "Sure does! Most people are discharged into treatment within 24-48 hours from submitting the referral, depending on what type of treatment is needed and if there is a bed available."

Next, they headed to the Palliative Care Unit. "We have Palliative Care today. I know you're familiar with that unit."

"Sure am. I would go see my grandma there almost every day after school. They are so nice there. Noella is an angel."

Unfortunately, when they got up there, Noella was not on today. A new receptionist was there instead. "This unit has the highest turnover rate for reception" Jacki said, as they walked to their first patient. "I think people don't realize how emotionally exhausting working on a floor that sees death really is."

Colleen agreed. "It's not for everyone, that's for sure. I seem to have a gift in that department. I was young when my grandpa died, but even then, I wanted to be by his side and help him, even if it was just getting him water or sitting with him." Jacki understood that. "I like this unit, myself. I wouldn't mind being assigned here. But I always saw myself as an ED chaplain. This would be my second choice, though. I always enjoy when I am assigned this floor." They had a few patients that were not interested in long visits, but one patient was lonely and welcomed having two ladies to talk to. After a few minutes of visiting, they closed the door and Colleen watched Jacki type her notes in. "Our last stop for the day is my unit, the ED. I just checked the board and it's unusually empty for a Friday afternoon, but we can pass through and see what's going on."

Jacki was happy to see Sara was working today. "Hi Sara! This is my shadow for the day, Colleen. I saved the ED for last. How is it down here? Is the board down? Or is what I'm seeing accurate?" Sara had to laugh. "I know, I can't believe it either. But, yes, what you see is what's here. I'm not sure I trust it, but we'll go with it for now." Colleen observed as Jacki went in and made the referral for hospice for an elderly gentleman with end-stage CHF. The family accepted the decision, and Fred would be transferred to Alisha's hospice agency within the next few hours. Jacki then popped in to visit some patients there for routine injuries, and a few pneumonia cases that were awaiting a bed on the Respiratory unit.

"Well, that's a wrap." Jacki said. "Now, let's go get an ice cream and have a chat."

"I never say no to ice cream!" Colleen said. They took their ice cream to Jacki's office, so they could talk quietly. Colleen's eyes fell on the basketball. "Did you play basketball? Who's Jeffrey?" Jacki smiled. Alisha could always share her story of meeting Gracie, and now Jacki could share the story of Jeffrey.

"Do you remember, a few months ago, hearing about a school bus accident?"

"Oh gosh! Yes, the drunk truck driver! Was Jeffrey the boy that was injured?"

"There were a few injuries that day, but Jeffrey took the brunt of it, as the truck went on his side of the bus. He lost both his legs. He was the star basketball player for the Puppington Corgis. He surprised me at his championship game by being able to play thanks to a specially designed wheelchair. He gifted me the signed basketball at his game."

"That is awesome. So, you have a chance to make a difference in a lot of lives as a chaplain, huh?"

"Yes, you do. Some patients, you won't remember once you walk away. But other times, they stick with you. Their story, their lesson---you will never forget them. I kept in contact with

Jeffrey, and I'm taking the next few days off to attend his trial proceedings."

"I hope that drunk driver gets a lot of time behind bars. He's lucky nobody lost their life." Jacki nodded. "So, what did you think, Colleen? Would you be interested in an internship this summer? Do you have any questions?"

"I would love an internship! I love how advanced Mount Mercy is, and their service reaches even those who society frowns upon. The definition of mercy. I guess my only question would be how you got into the field." Jacki sighed. "I should have known that question would come up. I honestly don't have a fancy, life changing story, like some do. I, just like you, have always been compassionate. Had a knack for the elderly and the dying. and wanted to do something that would change their lives at that moment. My pastor set me up with a job shadow, and it clicked. They hired me on the spot and now I'm the ED chaplain, and soon to be the Director of Spiritual Care. On a personal note, though, I like to think my daughter Melanie led me spiritually to this point. I lost her a few years ago, while I was still pregnant. After her birth, I found out I cannot have any more children, so it hasn't been an easy road. But Mount Mercy is a family, and they've stood by me as I've grown and peeled off layers of healing. I baptized Sara a few months ago, after she came to me for Spiritual guidance."

"WOW! That must have been amazing. Do you see yourself adding to your ministry, outside of Mount Mercy?" Jacki thought for a moment. That question threw her off guard. "I'm not sure. I mean, I've thought about going back to school for Ministry, I could see myself as a pastor. But I love my patients. And the connections I make with them. I guess I'll have to revisit that question later."

They finished their ice creams and Jacki walked Colleen to the main entrance. "I see you survived" Stella yelled out. "I sure did, Stella. And I'm pretty sure you'll be seeing more of me around here. So, look out!" Jacki couldn't help but laugh. "Ouch. Those are fighting words, Stella. You may have met your match."

"Eh, If I can shut you down with my sarcasm, I can handle another one."

"Ouch. That was a little rough, there, Stella" Jacki said with a smile. She grabbed her keys and headed home herself. She was off this weekend and took the first half of the week off for Jeffrey's trial. She went home and headed for a warm bubble bath to start her self-care weekend.

Chapter 15

Jacki enjoyed a quiet weekend with her dog. She was proud of herself for relaxing and "doing nothing" for a change. She went to church on Sunday with Sara, and they went to lunch afterwards, but other than that, it was a quiet weekend at home doing whatever she felt led to do. The first two days of Jeffrey's trial were intense and filled with witnesses, evidence, and investigation photos.

Today was the last day of the trial, ending with the jury deliberating and hopefully reaching a verdict. They had the accident photo on display in front of the court room. When Jacki saw the damage to the school bus, her eyes filled with tears. Other members of the team that were on the bus also came, a few of them were able to get up and speak about what they saw.

The truck driver's attorney was trying to downplay the entire event, saying he was not drunk, but asleep at the wheel. The prosecutor did not have any of it. Jacki felt like she was watching a tennis match and couldn't help but smile.

"In this instance, attorney, rather your client was asleep at the wheel, stoned, or highly intoxicated, which scientific evidence in the form of blood and urine samples, were presented that show your client's blood alcohol level was FOUR times the normal limit. Not two times, or three…. FOUR times over the normal limit, regardless of the circumstances and which are correct in your findings, the damage was still done. Your client is lucky that none of the children or staff on the bus were killed. How you can ignore the scientific medical proof that your client was severely under the influence, and driving a company truck, to boot, when this accident occurred is beyond me."

The attorney continued to argue, stating their client had medications that could cause those levels to rise, however could not produce a list of said medications to the judge and jury. Suddenly the judge had had enough.

"There will be no more fighting or pointless arguing in this court room. You are both acting like children at recess, in front of a panel of jurors, family members of the victims, and other members of the court and media outlets covering this case. It ends right this minute. Before we dismiss the jury, I am calling Jeffrey to the stand."

Jeffrey rolled up to the front with his wheelchair, which they had prepared a lowered microphone, so he did not have to leave his wheelchair.

Code Mercy

"Thank you, your honor for this time. This trial, and the event that happened has taken its toll on my family. I wanted to speak directly to you, Mister Picorelli. You have changed my life forever. Although none of my classmates were injured, you have changed their lives too. We were all members of the basketball team. We were returning home from a field trip when you slammed your truck into us. I was their star player. Now I have no legs. My dreams of joining the NBA were crushed. I will never get to walk down the aisle, or dance at prom, or take my dog for a run on my own legs again. Modern technology has allowed people to play basketball in specially powered wheelchairs, and there are prosthetics, but that will never be the same. I am only 13, sir. I should still have my legs and be enjoying the upcoming summer vacation with my friends. Instead, I endure multiple doctors' visits in a week, extensive physical therapy to strengthen my arms who now must operate a wheelchair, and am unable to do basic functions, like go to the bathroom as I need to. My teammates lost their star basketball player. Yes, my wheelchair allows me to play, but not in the capacity I, or they, are used to. We still won the state championship, but they felt this tragedy just as much as myself and my family have. Your selfish decision to drink that much and then get behind the wheel has caused all of this to happen. Before the jury deliberates, and regardless of the outcome, I have chosen to speak to you in front of everyone today, to say I forgive you. Whatever you're going through in your personal life that caused you to drink enough to be four times over the legal limitations for driving, means you are going through something serious yourself. Or perhaps, you just don't care about other people when you're drinking. Whatever your reasonings, I hope the results of this trial allow you time to think, reflect, and work on yourself."

Jeffrey rolled his wheelchair back to where his parents were sitting. Jacki couldn't believe how strong Jeffrey was at that moment. *That's one tough kid. I don't think I could forgive him, if it were me,* she thought to herself. Jacki looked around the room, nearly everyone was crying or sniffling. Jeffrey's words were impactful. The defendant, of course, was expressionless, which irritated Jacki to her core. The jury was dismissed, and everyone inside the court room waited anxiously for what Jacki hoped was a quick verdict. She decided to go talk to Jeffrey and his parents.

"That was amazing, Jeffrey. And so strong of you to forgive him for his actions."

Jeffrey smiled. "Thanks, Jacki. I just felt like Jesus would want me to forgive him. It doesn't mean what he did was okay, or that

I'll ever forget what happened---I can't. I'll remember every time I look down and see no legs. But it frees me from the bitterness and allows me to move forward, with the limitations I now must endure." Jacki had no words; she just shook her head in amazement. The sun was shining so she opted to take a walk. As she was exciting the courtroom, she noticed her sister Amy sitting in the other corner with her cameraman. She seemed busy, so Jacki decided not to bother her. She would catch her after the verdict.

After nearly three hours of waiting, the jury filed back into the courtroom with their verdict. Jacki anxiously tried to read their facial expressions but was unable to find any that pointed in one direction or another. *A strict poker face must be a requirement of a jury member,* she thought to herself. This wasn't Jacki's first rodeo in a court room, so she knew the rules of how the verdict was read. She waited patiently, as the prosecution team, then the attorney and the defendant filed back into the courtroom.

"Ladies and gentlemen, the jury has a verdict." The chosen jury member began. "In the case of State vs. Picorelli, the jury finds Antonio Picorelli guilty of negligence behind the wheel of a deadly vehicle, and guilty of driving while intoxicated using a company vehicle."

The courtroom came alive with reactions. Many were crying, the team members were high fiving each other and rallying around Jeffrey and his family in support. Jacki could not suppress the excitement that she felt inside of her. GUILTY. This verdict would not change the outcome of Jeffrey's life. He will still never walk on his own legs again, never be able to take a shower by himself. Never jump to score a basket, or dive into the swimming pool. But this verdict, and Jeffrey being able to forgive him, would allow Jeffrey to heal and begin another piece of this journey---acceptance.

The judge then addressed those in attendance, specifically speaking to Antonio. "You, sir, in my opinion, are a very evil, selfish man. You were driving your company's 18-wheeler, under FOUR TIMES the legal amount of alcohol. Those 18-wheelers are strong on their own, but when you add an under the influence driver to their gas pedal, you become a homicide weapon. You better count your lucky stars that none of these precious children, or their staff members were killed. Jeffrey, you are one amazing young man, to forgive this man for taking the remainder of your childhood away, as you knew it. At the age of 13, you now must be assisted by your parents, a specially assigned teacher, and countless medical personnel throughout your day. Because this man chose to drive his big truck while intoxicated. This, personally, is the most difficult and disgusting case I have ever seen. You, Antonio Picorelli, are hereby sentenced to 40 years in the state prison. Your parole eligibility will be discussed at a further date, but for now, 40 years in the state prison is what you will face. In my opinion, that is nowhere near enough. Court is dismissed, get out of my courtroom you vile man." The judge banged her gavel, and the security guards escorted him out a side door, while others filed out the main doors. Jacki stayed behind, to observe and listen to the sounds of a guilty verdict. Jacki went to visit an old friend from high school who worked as a court clerk and noticed her sister Amy standing outside doing her live shot, as she was planning to leave. She decided to stay until Amy was finished before walking over. "This is Amy Redmond reporting live from the Puppington County Court House, WWJD 7."

Once Amy was done, and her cameraman began putting their tools away, Jacki approached Amy and tapped her on the shoulder.

"Still the best reporter in the state, sis." Jacki said, as Amy turned around.

"Jacki! What are you doing here?" Amy seemed surprised to see her sister.

"I took care of Jeffrey as a chaplain the day of his accident. He and his family mean a lot to me, so I took the three days off to attend his trial and support them."

There was silence between the two of them, so Jacki decided to break it. "Amy, I just want to say I'm sorry. We've grown apart the last couple years. After I lost Melanie. It's been so hard for me, and I just felt you didn't understand. A lot of people can't, but instead of accepting that I pulled away. I'm sorry."

Amy appeared irritated for a few minutes, and Jacki prepared for the worst. She prepared to hear her sister reply with a negative response to her apology. Instead, Jacki got one of her own.

"Jacki—don't apologize. If anyone should be apologizing, it's me. I'm your older sister. There are a few years between us, but that is just a number. We were close before, but I couldn't accept who you wanted to be. I was so high up in my own world of being on TV that I let that get in the way of being supportive of my little sister, who wanted to serve others in their time of need. And you're right, I also wasn't there for you when you lost Melanie. I'm sorry, Jacki. I hope you can be as merciful as Jeffrey and let me be your sister again. The close knit, loving sisters we once were, before TV fame sucked me in and I became an arrogant, self-centered person, at your expense."

Jacki hugged Amy so tightly, and Amy returned the hug. They were both wiping away tears as they pulled back. "I absolutely can forgive you, Amy. I've missed you. There's so much you've missed out on. I know our career paths are total opposites, but we are both happy, and that is what truly matters. Mount Mercy has its award banquet on Friday night, if you'd like to go."

"Of course, I wouldn't miss that for the world, now that I have my sister back in my life, who works for such a great hospital. And I promise I will come as myself, as your sister, and not as the news reporter looking for a good story." They both shared a giggle and one additional hug, before Jacki left to join Jeffrey, his family, and the team for a picnic lunch at the school field.

Jacki's Thursday at work was uneventful, giving her lots of time to prepare for tomorrow's banquet. Even though she had the first half of the week off for Jeffrey's trial, Kathryn insisted Jacki be off on the day of the banquet. This made Jacki curious, but she went with it. Kathryn had been a wonderful boss to Jacki, she would be sad to see her go. Once she had finished her rounds, she stopped by Kathryn's office. When she came in, she noticed

Kathryn quickly shuffle some papers to cover whatever she was writing.

"Hello there! Done already?" Kathryn said in a rushed tone. Jacki was suspicious now but was not one to ruin surprises. She also didn't want to be disappointed if she in fact was not getting an award. "Yeah, basic day today. SUD unit is a little slow lately, huh?"

"Yes, our numbers in that unit have been low lately. But I guess that could be a good thing. I'm sure they will rise again with the summer heat approaching."

"True. Are you ready for the banquet? Your last one, I bet it feels bittersweet."

Kathyn sighed. "It does and it doesn't. I have loved my job for the last 40 years and have made many of these speeches. They're time consuming, but I somehow will still miss them. I'll miss seeing other staff members dressed up, and catching up with people I don't see often. But I won't miss dressing up. I hate dress shopping!"

Jacki snickered. "Same here, girl. This is my first one, so I don't know what to expect or even what you're talking about, when you say you gave many speeches. Does each unit give a speech?"

Kathryn had a panicked look on her face, as if she realized she had nearly given away a surprise. "Uh, well. It's always good to have a speech on hand, in case you win an award, you know" she laughed anxiously. Jacki nodded suspiciously to herself but kept on listening. "Well, I'll let you get back to your speech. I just wanted to stop by and say hello, since I'm not here tomorrow. I know we'll be seeing more of each other in the coming weeks, but I just wanted to say thank you, Kathryn. It's been such an honor to have you as my boss. I've learned all I know about patient care, compassion, and how to minister to different people, from you. You took a chance to hire me with no other background other than my education, when I'm sure other candidates had better qualifications. It means the world to me that you trusted me that much, and with so much in the future."

Kathryn sighed shakily. "Jacki---I did what I did because I saw more within you, than you did yourself. I saw that you had love in your heart. I knew you'd been through stuff, even though you hadn't shared it yet. Those painful experiences in our own lives bring out the compassion and love that others need. That's not something you can learn in a textbook. Was it a risk? Of course.

But it paid off in a huge way, both for you, and for Mount Mercy. Now go on, get to your station in the ED and finish out your day, then go give yourself a manicure or something, would you?" Jacki smiled as she hugged Kathryn. The ED was unusually slow, and Sara had the afternoon off. She hung out with Angelina, the lab tech assigned to the ED. Not many people liked her, because she was 'out there', but Jacki enjoyed talking with her. They had different belief systems, but recognized and respected each other's choices. She was called into a patient room to facilitate a transfer to comfort care, and visited an elderly lady who had broken a hip and was lonely, before heading home.

Jacki had a hair and nail appointment for 10 Friday morning. Sandie had insisted that she treat herself to a full package to go with her fancy awards dress. Although Jacki was not one for vanity, she had to admit she was excited. For her hair, she opted for a fancy up-do, and for her nails, she opted for a shade lighter than her dress. Sandie was coming over at 3 that afternoon, with Alisha, to help her get into her dress and do her makeup.

"Hello ladies!" Jacki said, as she answered the door. "It's not a wedding, but let's pretend, shall we?" Everyone laughed. Jacki poured them each a glass of wine and had a spread of cheese and crackers on the table for them to snack on while working on her dress and makeup.

"Are you nervous?" Sandie asked. "This is the first big event you've gone to."

"To be honest, I am a little nervous. I saw Kathryn working on something yesterday when I stopped in to talk to her. And a few weeks ago, I was talking with Sara, and she looked like she was going to say something but stopped herself."

Alisha looked at Jacki. "Are you winning an award? That would be awesome."

"I'm starting to wonder. But I'm not one to ruin surprises. If I'm honored with an award, great, if not that's okay too. I'm just glad you're both going to be there."

"Did you invite anybody else?" Sandie asked, as she fastened the last button on Jacki's dress.

"My sister Amy is coming. As herself, not as a news reporter. I know Sara is coming, as she always goes to represent the ED. Other than that, I don't know."

They continued getting ready. Alisha did Jacki's makeup, before getting her dress on. Both she and Sandie also got dresses, although not as fancy as Jacki's. Sandie chose a beautiful lilac colored dress, and Alisha had chosen a long black skirt with a red sequined top. "I don't do dresses, unless it's a funeral." Alisha said with a laugh. "Skirts can be just as elegant if you know how to pair them." Jacki nodded in agreement. "You both look beautiful! Shall we head out?" They looked at the time and agreed it would be a good time to leave. The awards ceremony started at 7, but everyone was encouraged to arrive around 5, for cocktail hour and socializing. They took Sandie's car, as it was slightly bigger. The event was being held at the Puppington Country Club, on the property of a beautiful meadow with a view of the mountains. Jacki had to admit it was nice to see everyone dressed up. They found their seats and ordered their drinks from the bar.

Jacki surprised herself, as she started walking around introducing herself to random people that she may have only seen in passing. Kathryn, any chance she got, would introduce her as the upcoming Director of Spiritual Care, which made Jacki blush. Although she was excited to take the position, all the attention would be a learning curve for Jacki.

The two hours before the ceremony went by quickly, and the president of the medical center got up first to address everyone. Slowly, each unit or specialty that had an award would get up and present an award. It was done at random, so Jacki had no idea what unit would be mentioned next. Suddenly, Kathryn got up. Jacki began to get anxious, but still would not let herself believe it could possibly be her. She listened intently to Kathryn's speech.

"The dictionary defines a chaplain as a member of an institution, organization, unit in the armed forces, or a medical facility that guides and encourages in matters of faith. Here at Mount Mercy, we are known for our over-the-top compassion in Spiritual Care. Tonight's honoree takes the definition of chaplain and raises it to the max. This person has only been with the program a few years. She has faced many hardships in her personal life, which she brings to the bedside of a variety of patients. What makes this person unique, compared to our other chaplains, is her fierce love for each patient. She loves them with the heart of Christ. Once they are released from the hospital, this chaplain still reaches out to them. She has taught a young boy how to forgive someone who altered his life. She stood by the bedside of the young and old alike, as they took their last breath. She held hands and cried with grieving parents, as they welcomed a child with no breath. She has advocated for one of our grieving mothers, when a doctor was being disrespectful and unethical. She has supported the first-in-the-state SUD unit within Mount Mercy, treating patients with addictions and releasing them to specialized treatment centers, giving them a chance to regain their lives after submitting to substance abuse and drug use. She has advocated for the patients in our psychiatric unit, including one young patient who did not belong in the unit to begin with. On top of her patient work, this chaplain also has captured the hearts of other co-workers, from unit secretaries and receptionists, to nurses, doctors, and environmental staff. She has even saved the life of one of our support staff during a mental health crisis, resulting in the adaptation of 'code mercy', to be used in every mental health situation in the ED. This person has gone above and beyond her call of duty, and I am pleased to present this award, of Chaplain of the Year, to Jacki Redmond, the new Director of Spiritual Care."

The entire room started cheering, and many staff members were on their feet, yet Jacki remained seated. It had not hit her yet, that Kathryn was speaking about her. Alisha jabbed her in the shoulder "get up, goof nut! She was talking about you!" Suddenly, Jacki looked on the stage, and realized every single one of her special patients were there---Jeffrey, Veronica, Marc, Emma's parents, Suzie, Maggie, Sara, Colleen… Jacki couldn't believe her eyes. They flooded with tears, as she got up and made her way, shakily, to the platform to accept her award. A woman of comedy on the side, Jacki started her speech with a laugh. "Well, I guess Kathryn was right when she said to always have a speech prepared. I truly do not know what to say right now. This is not what I expected at all. I refuse to follow the usual format the movie stars use, thanking their parents, their dog, their friends, and family---instead. I choose to thank these people spread out before me. Each one of you represents the hundreds of patients I have served over my past few years here. I met each of you in various situations---some were tragic, others were just a part of life that I had the chance to be present for. This is what a chaplain does. A chaplain serves their patients and their families. The opportunity doesn't always present itself to continue contact with them after they are a patient here at Mount Mercy. But, when they do, I continue to support them. I thank you, Kathryn, and everyone here at Mount Mercy, for making me feel so welcomed, and preparing and equipping and supporting me as I embark on this new journey as Director of Spiritual Care. And I thank the Good Lord above, for allowing me to go through what I went through to get here today. There were times in my life where I did not know what my next minute would look like, yet he walked beside me and pulled me through. I thank you all and look forward to serving hundreds more of our patients, together with the rest of Mount Mercy staff."

Jacki stepped off the platform, hugging each of those who had made their way to the stage to surprise her. On her way back to her seat, she met with others who wanted to give her a hug. Waiting for her at her table was her sister. Dressed in a beautiful sparkling blue gown, holding their favorite photo of them both, and a bouquet of flowers. At this moment, Jacki mentally took a step back, to take this all in.

Every single one of the people on that stage had a message. Even those in the seats, that chose not to be recognized, also stood for a message of mercy. Jacki had learned the many levels of forgiveness---it's not just an "I'm sorry." You sometimes deserve an apology, but never get it. You may be faced with a life altering event, or perhaps the loss of a loved one, from someone else's careless actions. You may need to forgive someone who has already passed, or is now in their final days, which feels unfair since you have lived years with the hurt, they caused. Sometimes, you even need to show yourself a little mercy. Jacki learned, and assisted, in all these lessons in her past two years at Mount Mercy. She even began the process of forgiving herself for the difficult losses in her own life. But today, as she leaned into the open arms of her sister, she realized one important lesson of mercy---

sometimes forgiveness happens at the perfect time and allows you to reunite with someone you have missed.

She wrapped her arm around her sister and looked around at everyone here to celebrate her and the other honorees. This was Mount Mercy. This was the Medical Center of the next century, the Medical Center with first-in-the-state units, and top-rated Spiritual Care. A unit which she would shortly be the Director of. She smiled as she raised a glass of wine with those around her table.

Perhaps Esther had it right. Perhaps this is the moment for which Jacki was created. (Esther 4:14)

Special Thanks:

There are a few people I must thank at the end of this book. First and foremost, God above, for inspiring me, giving me the vision for the theme and the characters, who all rallied under the same mission and message, to create such an amazing story.

Secondly, to my best friend and spiritual soulmate, Pauline, who acted as editor, and supported and stood by this book's message from the beginning, even when its message was under attack. Pauline is also responsible for the author's photo on the back cover.

Lastly, Robin, for bringing my cover idea to life, and making it more beautiful than I could ever imagine or create on my own.

Code Mercy